Go To Helena Handbasket

Donna Moore was born in 1962 and led a sheltered childhood in a small English village. A crime fiction fan from a young age, Donna wanted to be one of Enid Blyton's Famous Five and fight crime with the aid of only a basket of cucumber sandwiches and a bottle of ginger beer. She spent her spare time following mysterious strangers around the village—especially those with cockney accents and a couple of days' growth of stubble—until a complaint from the new local vicar put a stop to her sleuthing career.

She now lives in Glasgow, where she has a thrilling dual career as a mild-mannered pension consultant by day, and an unemployed superhero by night. For relaxation she listens to Dean Martin and The Ramones, watches screwball comedy and film noir, and enjoys salsa, cha cha cha and merengue—despite having two left feet. ...*Go To Helena Handbasket* is her first book.

Go To Helena Handbasket

POINTBLANK

Cover photograph by Jacob Appelbaum
jacob@appelbaum.net | www.appelbaum.net

Book design by oiva design group | oivas.com

Set in Caslon

POINTBLANK is an imprint of Wildside Press
www.pointblankpress.com
www.wildsidepress.com

Series Editor JT Lindroos
Editor Allan Guthrie

For more information contact Wildside Press

To Mum, Dad, Darren, and John

Acknowledgments:

More thanks than I can possibly express coherently go to Al 'Sunshine' Guthrie and JT Lindroos; to my fellow PointBlankers and friends Ray 'Kuncklebuster' Banks, Duane 'Leblanc' Swierczynski and Anthony Neil Smith; and to Ken Bruen, Barbara Seranella, Sally Cadagin, Bobbie Rudd, Sherry Sharp and Maddy Van Hertbruggen. Love and huge hugs to you all for your help, friendship and support. And to everyone on 4MA and RAM— thank you for all your suggestions for cliches, and for your encouragement. Thanks all. I owe you a drink.

PROLOGUE

(Why The Hell Isn't This Called Chapter 1?)

If I was going to become a serial killer, I needed to learn more about the job.

I'd bought a copy of Serial Killing For Dummies *on eBay from a Seller called RitualSlasher. He was selling his entire book collection because he was 'going away for at least 25 years.' I'd thanked him for the book and told him I hoped he had a lovely time on his vacation.*

I couldn't help thinking that one day, I, too, might be able to give up serial killing and enjoy my dried, cured and well-preserved memories.

The book wasn't in the 'excellent' advertised condition. Rusty brown stains were dotted throughout, and there was a pervasive coppery smell. But what annoyed me most was a leathery object bookmarking the chapter entitled: 'Collecting Tokens From Your Victims And How To Store Them So They Don't Rot.' I couldn't work out if the bookmark had started life as a rasher of bacon, or an ear.

Putting both my irritation and the bookmark to one side, I opened the book at the first chapter, 'Your Childhood: It Was Really, Really Bad'. All I could remember of my own childhood were endless lazy summer days when my parents and two older sisters would spoil me rotten with toys, picnics, ice cream, trips to the park, holidays at the seaside. I ran wild in our huge garden, climbed trees, caught tadpoles in the nearby river, and made a den in the woods where I crocheted tea-cosies for the village fête and pressed my collection of woodland flowers—typical boy stuff.

No, I'd repressed the darker side of my hideous childhood for too long and I wasn't prepared to allow those horrific events to remain buried deep in my warped psyche a minute longer. Perhaps my evil parents had brainwashed me. If I was to have any sort of future as a serial killer, I needed to find out the truth. Right now.

I reached for the phone.

"Hello, Mum."

"Darling, how are you?"

"I'm trying to remember my traumatic childhood, bitch. Can you give me some pointers?"

"You had a lovely *childhood, dear. You were a very good little boy."*

"*Come clean now, Mum. Tell me about the bedwetting, the arson, how I used to torture cats and rabbits and the next-door neighbour's pet guinea pig. I bet I was sent to a reformatory when I was eight.*"

"*Oh no, dear. You were in Mrs Povey's class at St David's Primary School For Dear Little Boys. Don't you remember the Christmas Pageant? Everyone said they'd never seen such an angelic looking Angel Gabriel.*"

"*Ah! Ritualistic satanic abuse. That was your bag, was it?*"

"*Sweetheart, have you been drinking?*"

I pounced on that one. "*Oh yes, and talking about drinking, Mother, you and Father were raving alcoholics, weren't you? I can almost remember. You destroyed my childhood with your drunken rages and alcohol-fuelled fights.*"

"*But, darling, you know Daddy only drinks that lovely Elderflower wine he makes in the shed, and I have my single glass of dry sherry at New Year.*"

Hmmm. I could see it was going to be hard to prise the truth out of Mumsie. "*What about pets? You never let me have any pets, did you? What was it—did you come across me ripping the legs off a spider?*"

"*Sweetheart, you had a dear little bunny when you were six and when it died you were so distraught your father and I agreed we would spare you that pain again.* That's *why we didn't have any pets afterwards. Don't you remember the ceremony we had for Flopsy? You read out a lovely poem you'd written.*"

"*But how did Flopsy die, Mother? I killed him, didn't I? Killed him in a particularly nasty way involving scalpels and an iron, isn't that right?*"

"*He died of old age, darling. He had a good long life and died peacefully in his sleep with a smile on his little whiskery face.*"

"*Aha! That's exactly what you said about Grandad. I knew there was something odd about his death. Stop lying to me, Mother. Tell me about the fires. Did I set fire to the school? Did you find a stockpile of matches and petrol in my bedroom? Was I unnaturally drawn to firemen?*"

"*You* did *get your Camping Badge when you were in the Boy Scouts. I think that to get the badge you had to make a fire by rubbing two sticks of wood together. Although . . .*"

This was it! She was finally going to reveal the terrible, evil deed of my childhood that would give me the key to unlock the padlock on the door through which serial killers entered a world of pain and blood. Yep, this would make me a proper serial killer. "*What, Mum?*"

"*Well, now you come to mention it, I do remember your Scout Leader telling me there was a nasty scene the day you took your Badge.*"

"*What was it, Mother? Did I threaten my little pals with a burning branch? Did I douse all the tents with my secret stash of petrol? Did I tell everyone they were*" going to burn in the fires of Hell, and that I was the Devil's satanic Zippo?"

"No, dear. You nearly failed that badge because you were afraid of the fire and wanted to come home to Mummy."

I put the phone down. It was pretty obvious that the evil she-devil who called herself my mother was keeping something from me. I had no doubts that my background fully qualified me as first-class serial killer material. And if anyone ever asked me for my qualifications, well, I could just make up some shit.

I was nearly there. I just needed to work on a signature. A poem written in my victims' blood left behind at the scene of each of my heinous crimes. Or orchid petals scattered around the freshly slaughtered body. Could I see myself carving the words of a Barry Manilow song on a pale, still chest—with a corkscrew? Did I even know the words to a Barry Manilow song? Or would that be too cruel, in any case?

I looked down at the hand on the table in front of me. I picked it up by the thumb, dropped it into the ice-filled picnic box, and forced the lid shut. How much more of a signature did I need?

CHAPTER ONE

(The Client, The Case, And A Recipe)

Of all the run-down, flea-bitten Private Investigator offices in all the UK, he had to walk into mine. I was sitting at the battered antique desk I'd won from a feisty old broad in a Poker tournament. Strictly speaking, it wasn't so much antique as just plain old; and, since we're fostering a spirit of honesty and openness here, it wasn't so much a Poker tournament as a game of Monopoly, and the feisty old broad was my mother. Anyway, business had been slower than a knee-capped snail with arthritis, which is why I was fashioning a facsimile of the Leaning Tower of Pisa out of paperclips while I wondered how I could possibly continue to stave off the moment when I'd have to tell my secretary, Fifi Fofum, she was fired.

We didn't have enough work to keep us both employed. In fact, we didn't have enough work to keep *one* of us employed. Since opening the office eight months ago I'd spent most of my time waiting for the phone to ring, and Fifi had passed her days trying to learn how to make a decent cup of coffee. Or 'Java', as she insisted on calling it. One of us had been reading too many pulp detective novels and both of us had drunk too much really awful coffee over the past few months.

Right now, Fifi was out of the office. She'd left, saying, "Gotta take a powder, sister. Got an appointment with the croaker and then I need to get some gaspers and some giggle juice." Frankly, I hadn't a clue where she'd gone. For once, the office was restful, and I was mulling over how I was going to drum up some business before I ran out of paperclips when a man walked through the door and shattered the peace. It wasn't just the peace that was shattered. The door was too. Probably because he hadn't bothered to open it.

The chipped black lettering in my frosted glass door read SNOITAGITSEVNI TEKSABDNAH ANELEH. Initially, I'd worried that I'd only get Czech clients, but then I realised I was sitting on the wrong side of the door and prospective clients would see the words HELENA HANDBASKET INVESTIGATIONS. Well, not any more they wouldn't. The glass was in shards all over the floor; the wooden doorframe was splintered and the hinges dangled.

"Come in," I said. "It's open."

The hulk stepped forward, crunching glass under his feet, and stopped at the edge of my desk. Given what he'd just done to the door, I was relieved he didn't walk through the desk too. He bent down and put hands the size of hams next to my telephone.

"My brother's," he said, his voice breaking in much the same way as the glass in my door. "These hands are my brother's. Find his killer and I'll give you eighteen thousand five hundred and forty-six pounds."

He leaned further forward and the stench of stale sweat shimmered in the air. He let out a breath that smelled as though a particularly skunky skunk had crawled into his mouth, got overexcited, and died. And not within the last week, either. His hair dripped grease like a badly fried burger, and his clothes were creased and stained, as though he hadn't changed them for a week.

Yes, yes, yes! This was a man I could really go for.

I pulled over a notepad and pen. "Tell me about your brother."

"His name's Robin. Robin Banks. He is . . . was . . . my older brother. I hadn't seen him for five years. Then these turn up on my front porch in a freezer box." He gestured to the hands on the desk, and I looked down at the pale but strangely hairy mitts, the knuckles tattooed in faded black ink: R O B I N B A N K S.

"And how do you know they're your brother's?"

He looked at me blankly.

I shrugged. "It might be a different Robin Banks."

"I know they're Robin's. We were very close."

"But you hadn't seen him for five years, Mr . . .?"

"Jeez—you sure you're a detective?" He pointed at the hands. "My brother was Mr Banks. *I'm* Mr Banks too." He held out a hand, which I shook and then yelped, wiping my palm on my t-shirt.

"Damn, sorry about that." He put the hand back down on the table and held out one of his own. "Owen," he said. "Robin's more intelligent, better looking brother."

I shook the hand. Based on the evidence before me, I couldn't vouch for the more intelligent, or better looking part, but his hand was definitely warmer than his brother's.

Owen Banks told me his brother's sorry story, how Robin had got mixed up with the local Stubezzi crime family when he was a teenager, and how he'd risen up the ranks to become Evan Stubezzi's right-hand man in a sort of 'local boy makes bad' way. I bit my tongue—God, it hurt. But it stopped me mentioning that Robin wasn't going to be anybody's right-hand or left-hand man from now on. I knew of Evan Stubezzi. He was untouchable. It was said that he had the cops in his pocket, although I couldn't figure out how, unless he wore enormous coats made of some superstrength material.

"Let me explain," Owen said. "Five years ago, there was this jewel heist. Evan Stubezzi has some seemingly legitimate business interests—all part of Stubezzi Enterprises. That's how he launders money from the less legitimate side of his empire. He had carried off this huge drug deal and he was going to launder thirty million pounds in cash by washing it through one of his subsidiaries, Stubezzi Jewellery. For months, Stubezzi had been planning the whole thing down to the smallest detail. Only he'd not factored in one thing. Robin. Stubezzi Jewellery took delivery of a large consignment of precious stones from Holland. Twelve hours later the jewels had disappeared. All thirty mills' worth of them. And so had Robin."

I nodded wisely. "Ah, so you think he ran off with the proceeds of the heist?" I asked, brilliantly.

Owen looked at me, bemused. "Are you *really* sure you're a detective? Sorry for sounding blunt, but you seem a bit slow on the uptake."

"Hey, big guy!" I pointed to the wall behind me. "Of course I'm a detective. What do you think all those certificates are? See that one—The FBI Surveillance Course? Got that just last week." Owen looked impressed. I hurried on. It probably wouldn't do to tell him that FBI stood for Filey Bureau of Investigation and that it had its headquarters in the spare room of a terraced house in the town of Filey in Yorkshire. FBI was owned by two elderly sisters who needed to supplement their pensions and who had access to a photocopier. I also thought it wise not to mention that the large, gold-embossed certificate in the centre of the display, proclaiming me as a 'Licensed Private Investigator' was purchased on the Internet for fifty dollars. They were having a 'three for the price of two sale' so I also had certificates at home confirming I was a Doctor of Nostrilology and a High Priestess of Sister Immaculata's Church of The Voice of The Lonely Goatherd Layeeodlayeeodlayheehoo.

"Well, anyway," Owen continued. "Shortly after Robin's disappearance, I received a Christmas card, which was odd in itself." I was about to ask him why when he said, "It was July 15th. Which just so happens to be Robin's birthday. It must have been from him. It said: 'Staying out of the heat. Pretty cool here, but no ice at present.' The 'no ice' was in capitals and underlined."

I looked puzzled. Well, I imagine I did. Certainly, my face felt as though it had formed a puzzled expression. "Well, there wouldn't have been that much ice around in July, would there?"

Owen Banks picked up my letter opener and started cleaning the dirt from under one of his brother's fingernails. "'No ice.' I took that to mean he didn't have the jewels. Or if he did, he was going to sit on them for a while."

I nodded knowingly, as though this whole conversation wasn't going completely over my head. "Did the card say anything else?"

"Happy Christmas. Joy to the world. All that shit."

I waited to see if this had some special significance too, but Owen just shrugged his shoulders.

"That was the last time I heard from him until a few days ago," he said.

I doodled a hurried sketch of a large, hairy hand on the notepad in front of me. "So, what do you think has happened to him?"

"I think Stubezzi's caught up with him, discovered he doesn't have the jewels, and killed him as a warning to whoever does."

I whistled nervously. Evan Stubezzi was known as 'The Undertaker'. He wasn't *actually* an Undertaker, but he'd buried a lot of people. Most of them without the benefit of a religious ceremony. From the trunk of a car. I was going to earn my money if I took this case on.

"I think this calls for some whisky." I opened the bottom drawer of my desk.

"Not for me, thanks," said Owen.

I opened the next drawer up. "Brandy? Gin? Tequila?"

Another shake of the head.

Top drawer. "Vodka? Bud? Cherry Brandy? Babycham?"

"Too early for me—but you go ahead."

I looked at my watch—10 am. Oh well, it was bound to be midnight somewhere in the world. I took an ounce of Kahlúa and poured it into a shot glass. I then poured an ounce of Bailey's Irish Cream over the back of a spoon into the glass, so that the Bailey's formed a separate layer. And I topped it all off with a layer of Grand Marnier. Owen was looking at me, horrified. "B-52," I said. "Cheers."

"I'm beginning to wonder whether I made a mistake in coming to you," said Owen. "Do you have a drink problem?"

"Yes, but it's OK. My secretary is out replenishing stocks so, once she comes back, problem solved."

Owen shook his head yet again. You know, you can really go off a man when he's too self-righteous. But when the man looked as hot as Owen Banks, I was prepared to forgive him the odd foible.

He ran his hand through his greasy mane of hair and continued with his story. After the Christmas card, Owen hadn't heard from Robin at all until a few days before the hands had turned up. Out of the blue, Owen had received a cryptic note in Robin's handwriting (presumably before those hands had been clumsily removed at the wrists):

Royal Flush. Wednesday. Midnight. Come alone.

Obviously a man of few words (and even fewer fingers).

"I've racked my brains and I just can't think what he's trying to tell me," said Owen. "And now it's Wednesday, it's 10 am, and I'm holding my brother's hands, and not in a good way."

"Don't the words 'Royal Flush' mean anything to you?"

"Not a damn thing. I've spent the last four days trying to think of something and I just can't. Please help me."

I thought for a moment, sipping my B-52. "OK, here's what I'll do," I said. "Let me speak to my computer whiz and see what we can turn up. You try and think some more about this Royal Flush thing—it must mean *something*. I'll meet you tonight at . . . say . . . 10 pm? Which pub do you drink in?"

"The Royal Flush. On Sleazy Street, Downtown."

"OK, I'll see you there later. I can't promise anything. This is a real puzzle. Just one thing—why don't you go to the police? Surely this is more a case for the cops?"

"I don't trust them. Besides, they wouldn't want to know. Suspected murder, thirty million in hot ice, a pair of severed hands. I mean, can you really expect them to be interested?"

"Perhaps you're right."

He stood up. It was as though a huge weight had been lifted from his shoulders. He crunched over the glass on the floor. I watched his buttocks as they wriggled like a bucket full of frisky eels in his shiny-bottomed trousers. Damn, he was a fine specimen of manhood. At the door he hesitated.

"After all this is over I'd like to buy you dinner."

"Sounds good," I said. "I haven't had a chance to go grocery shopping for about a month and I'm running short. All I've had to eat today is a lightly sautéed veal escalope in a *jus* of fresh peaches and rosemary, served with courgettes and grilled tomatoes and a crusty French stick still warm from the oven. Errr . . . will your wife be coming to dinner with us?"

He smiled and picked off some of the dried egg staining his shirt. "I'm not married. There's nothing wrong with me or anything—I've just never found the right woman. Anyway, until later then. See you in The Royal Flush." He stepped through the frame of the broken door and headed downstairs. Man, he was fine.

I could hear Fifi coming up the stairs, her stiletto heels pecking away on the concrete steps outside the office like a murder of hungry crows. Fifi always made me think of the movie *Whatever Happened To Baby Jane*. She looked like Joan Crawford, even down to those outrageous eyebrows; and she acted like Bette Davis at her most insane. I loved Fifi dearly, but she was definitely not normal. Her scarlet lips appeared round what was left of the doorframe, followed shortly after by the rest of her face. So that was what her visit to the 'croaker' was all about— her six-monthly collagen injections. I should have realised when her lips had begun to look more or less normal again in the last month that it was time for another dose of poison. OK, so sometimes I'm not very good at noticing stuff. Even a PI has to take some time off every now and again.

"Who was the big lug with the sour puss who just dusted out? He looked down on his uppers and shit outta luck. What was he, some sorta hatchet man?" She nodded her red beehive, backcombed to within an inch of its life, towards what was left of the door. "He the one who squirted metal and put daylight in the crib door?"

"Fifi, I have absolutely no idea what you just said, but if you're talking about the gentleman who just left, he's our new client. Well, strictly speaking, he's our very first and only client."

Fifi beamed and threw herself down into the chair Owen Banks had recently vacated. "Yeah? Hotsy-totsy. That's just spiffy, doll. He hand over the lettuce?"

My secretary was deranged. Did she think our new client was a grocery boy?

She must have noticed my bewilderment. She said, "You know, sweetstuff—lettuce—cabbage, dough, spinach . . ."

"Fifi, why would anyone bring salad vegetables to a detective agency?"

"No, doll—spondulix, rhino, moolah, geetus, some of the folding . . ." Fifi rubbed her thumb and first two fingers together, her long scarlet talons clicking like dangerous mini castanets. ". . . mazuma, scratch, sugar, dosh."

Light dawned. "Fifi, if you mean money, why don't you just say so? Yes. He's going to give us a pretty sizeable fee for what sounds like a nice easy job."

Had I but known what was in store, I wouldn't have been so confident.

CHAPTER TWO

(Friends In High Places)

Fifi was in the small anteroom, which contained her desk, a phone, computer, printer, photocopier, fax machine and coffee machine. I called to her through the open door. "You busy, Fifi?"

"Busier than a one-legged tap dancer, kitten. Busier than a hustler with two bunks. Busier than a man who's overdosed on Viagra at a nymphomaniacs' convention."

"All you needed to say was 'yes'."

"My tonsils are dry, so I'm making us a nice cuppa joe, dollface," she said.

The coffee machine was a gift from my ex-colleagues when I left the ranks of the salaried in order to branch out on my own. Other than the phone, it was the only piece of equipment Fifi attempted to use. It was one of those shiny stainless steel jobs that grinds the beans, froths the milk and makes perfect espresso and cappuccino. That was the theory, anyway. All Fifi had ever been able to coax from it was mug after mug of hot mud that tasted as though it had been filtered through a cowpat. The computer was still in its box, and the fax machine was being used as a display shelf for bottles of nail varnish. About 5 months ago, Fifi had lugged in an old typewriter that she'd found in a junkshop. "Look at this mill, babe. This is hitting on all eight. I'll be able to type up your letters on this, no probs." I'd taken that to mean that she was happy with her purchase.

Since then, the few letters I'd dictated—most of them pleas to the bank not to call in the loan, or to the electricity company not to cut us off—Fifi had pecked out on the ancient machine. I'd tried it once—it was an ordeal pressing each key hard enough. And I didn't know how Fifi managed with her nails. But for some reason it was really comforting to hear the clacking of the keys and the ding of the carriage return on the rare occasions when Fifi took her secretarial role seriously and did what I'd hired her to do. OK, so the letter C was missing, but Fifi was resourceful. She managed to rephrase all my correspondence, so that none of it contained a C. This wasn't without its difficulties—I guessed that if we ever had a potential client with a C in his name we'd have to turn him down, and my letters were all signed off 'Bye Doll', instead of 'Yours sincerely', but we muddled along.

I needed to find out everything I could about Evan Stubezzi. I took my address book out of the only drawer that didn't contain alcohol (it was a very small drawer) and turned to the entries under 'F': 'Friend who works for the Council', 'Friend who works for the hospital', 'Friend who works for the Department of Vehicle Licensing', 'Friend who works for the local newspaper', 'Friend who's a psychiatrist', 'Friend in the Hospital Admissions Department', 'Friend who's a dentist', 'Friend who works at Pizza Express,' etc. I was lucky to have such a lot of useful friends in high places. I ran my fingers down the page until I found 'Friend who's a computer geek', and picked up the phone, dialling the number of my best friend, computer geek Heidi Salami.

Heidi lived in a room in her parents' house, with the curtains permanently closed, only coming out to indulge her other passion— skateboarding. She wasn't fond of interacting with her fellow human beings and was much more comfortable with bytes and RAM and Darkslides and Nose Grinds—all of which sounded painful and slightly kinky. We had grown up together, so she had learned to tolerate me, even though we had little in common. When she answered the phone I could hear the clicking of the control pad and Lara Croft kicking ass in the background.

"Heidi, Helena here—sorry to interrupt you when you're so busy, but I need everything you can get me on someone called Evan Stubezzi."

"OK, Helena. I'll see what I can do. Let me just get Lara past this tiger." I heard the sound of growling and shooting and then it all fell silent, leaving only Heidi's stereo with Dean Martin crooning in the background. "OK, I'm back. It might take me a while to hack into the police and government computers. Hang on." I waited patiently. "Here you go," Heidi said. "Evan Stubezzi. Age: 49. Profession: crime lord. Current residence: 184 South Street, Wimbledon, which he bought for two hundred K in 1989. Has a holiday caravan in Camber Sands, Essex. Came 4th in the karaoke competition at the social club there in May, singing the Sid Vicious version of 'My Way'. Owes ten grand on his American Express card but just posted a cheque in the post-box on the corner of Ewell Street to pay it off in full. Served two years for fraud in Bedford jail in the late 1990s where he shared a cell with a pimp named Sugar. MI5 currently have a bug on his phone and an operative, Ben

Dover, is sitting outside his house right now in a blue Ford Mondeo, eating a cheese and pickle sandwich which his wife, Eileen, prepared for him last night. Stubezzi drives a two-year-old Ferrari Dino. Married, with three kids. His wife drinks like a fish and is having an affair with her chiropodist. Medical records show that Stubezzi was treated for crabs in 1973 when he was in the army and that he had a hernia operation in 2002. He's currently seeing a Dr Ed Zup and has been paying regular visits to him once every two weeks for the last three years. His records don't say why. He's got the DVD of Terminator 3 on order from Amazon and he's just let his gym membership lapse because he's installed a home gym in his basement. Dyes his hair 'Dangerous Crime Lord Bluish-black' from the latest in the Harmony range of colours and has a poodle with a weak bladder called Ronnie Biggs (that's the name of the poodle, not its bladder by the way—there's nothing here to say what the poodle's bladder is called). Favourite song: 'Police and Thieves' by The Clash; favourite colour: green; favourite flower: edelweiss."

I could hear Heidi tapping a few more keys in time with Dean Martin's 'Send Me The Pillow That You Dream On'. Despite her mathematical and computer mind, Heidi was a romantic at heart with a penchant for Dean Martin songs and Doris Day movies.

She continued, "I know that's not much to go on but it's all I could get at such short notice. I'll e-mail you a detailed report and include his bank account and mobile phone numbers, details of calls made in the last six months, copies of his passport and driver's licence etc., etc. Usual stuff."

"Thanks, Heidi. As you say, it's not much but at least it gives me something to work with."

I broke the connection but kept the receiver in my hand, thinking. Those visits to Dr Zup sounded interesting. I wondered what they were all about. My e-mail pinged. Heidi had sent the detailed report she'd promised and on it was a phone number for Dr Zup. I dialled it.

"Dr Ed Zup speaking."

"Ah, Dr Zup. I wonder if you can help me. I'm an unlicensed private eye and I need some information on one of your patients. An Evan Stubezzi."

"I'm sorry. I can't give you information on any of my patients, young lady. To do so would be a dreadful and unforgivable breach of patient confidentiality for which I could, and undoubtedly *should*, get struck off. Apart from the professional considerations, I would never be able to live with myself if I broke a trust in that manner. No, no. A thousand times no."

"Oh, pleeeeease. It's really, really, really important."

"Well . . ."

"Pretty please?"

"OK. If it's *that* important. What do you need to know?"

It turned out that Dr Zup was a psychiatrist and he'd been treating Evan Stubezzi for insomnia. During hypnosis, Stubezzi had confessed to the drug deal and the fact that he'd surmised that Robin Banks had run off with thirty million pounds worth of jewels representing the ill-gotten gains from his, Stubezzi's, criminal activity. Stubezzi had also said on several occasions during the sessions that he had been trying to trace Robin Banks ever since. Dr Zup felt that this search was Stubezzi's driving force and that he couldn't rest until he'd found Banks. At the most recent session, Stubezzi had said that he was now sleeping more easily and wouldn't be needing Dr Zup any more. He'd found Robin Banks.

As an aside, Dr Zup revealed that he was also treating Evan Stubezzi for an irrational pathological fear of buttons. Dr Zup was worried because he didn't feel that Stubezzi had been completely cured. Slowly, the psychiatrist had been exposing Stubezzi to buttons, but by the time of the most recent session, Evan Stubezzi was still having all his clothes especially made with zips.

"He can be reduced to a gibbering wreck, just by showing him one of those double-breasted jackets with the shiny buttons," said Dr Zup. "I've never come across a case quite like it."

"Thanks, Doc," I said. "That's fascinating, although I don't suppose it will do me much good. However, I'll bear it in mind, just in case. And don't worry—I won't misuse or abuse the information you've given me."

I referred back to my address book and called a really good friend who works for the local newspaper.

"Good morning, Post and Courier, Barnaby Wilde speaking."

"Hi, Barnaby, mate. Helena here. How are you doing?"

"I'm sorry, miss, who did you say was calling?"

"Your good friend, Helena. Helena Handbasket."

There was silence on the other end of the phone. "I'm sorry, miss, I don't know anyone called Helena. Are you sure you have the right person? My name's Barnaby Wilde, just in case you misheard me."

"Of course I have the right person, Barnaby. We met in the produce aisle at Safeway's a couple of months ago. You were buying fruit and I asked you if I could squeeze your plums. You backed away, fell over your shopping trolley and your wallet fell out. I picked it up and returned it to you."

"Christ—yeah, I remember you. But how did you know my name and where I work?"

"Well . . ." I hesitated slightly. "Before I gave your wallet back I checked nothing had been stolen—you know, while you were temporarily concussed when your head hit the floor anybody could have helped themselves to your credit cards or that rather fetching photo of you wearing a leotard—I *love* wrestling—and I took one of your business cards so I could get in touch with you to make sure you were okay. Besides, you never can tell when knowing someone with the ability to do a Full Nelson, or a Cross-Face Chicken Wing Frankensteiner Frog Splash will come in useful."

"Bloody hell. 'Fetching', huh? Thanks. And I'm fine. What do you *really* want?"

"I need your help. I'm looking for articles about a big jewel heist five years ago. There were rumours that the Stubezzi gang was involved. Do you remember?"

"Yeah. You can get all this stuff at the library, you know. They have it all on computer. I can't help you I'm afraid—I'm really busy reporting on this serial killer case."

"What serial killer case?"

"You know—this one with the handless bodies dumped in woodland clearings. The bodies have had a Bible passage stuffed in their mouths and a scarlet-coloured fish sewn into their chest cavities. The police aren't telling the Press what the Bible quote is, and I'm trying to find out. So I just don't have the time to do anything for you, Eleanor."

"It's Helena. Oh, go on, pleeeeeeeeeeeeeeeease help."

"Well . . . alright then. As long as you promise *never* to contact me again."

"Anything you say, Barnaby. And hey, maybe we could meet up for a drink once this is all over. Maybe you could show me how to do the Spinning Gorilla Press Bodyslam. I'll give you a call." I gave him my snail mail and e-mail addresses to send the articles to and put the phone down.

Fifi brought me in a fresh cup of java and I told her everything I'd learned so far. But I was distracted. There was something niggling away in the back of my mind. Something someone had said to me today was really, really important. I just couldn't recall what it was. I knew it would come back to me at some point. I just hoped it wouldn't be too late.

CHAPTER THREE

(Product Placement, Irrelevant Filler, and Crime-Solving Cats)

I decided to go home and have a little nap on my Silentnight bed and see if I could work out what it was that was nagging away at my brain. I slipped into my Evans jacket which was hanging over the back of my chair, glanced down at my Timex watch and called out to Fifi. "I'm off to my Barrett Home. I'll be back in a couple of hours."

Fifi came out of her cubbyhole, blowing on her nails, which had been given a fresh coat of Revlon nail varnish. "That's jake, dollface. You just agitate the gravel and drift. If I catch any rumble I'll get you on the blower."

I had no idea what she just said. "Fifi, if you hear any news, give me a call."

I ran down the stairs, out of the Dulux post-box red door at the bottom and into the car park, where my 1974 Volkswagen Beetle was waiting for me. I drove home via the Johnson's Dry Cleaners to pick up my Warehouse suit, calling at Dunkin Donuts as I passed to pick up two dozen assorted donuts for breakfast, and finally pulled in to the kerb by my freshly Ronsealed fence.

I got out of the car, picked up my shopping and walked up the path, fishing my Yale key out of my handbag from Big Malc's market stall, where Big Malc himself worked while his wife sat on an orange plastic IKEA chair and kept a watch out for the cops.

"Hi, Virgil, I'm home."

Virgil perched on the living room windowsill, sunning himself. He looked up from licking his nether regions—a trick I had long been envious of—and jumped down to see if I would fill his bowl with Whiskas Meaty Chunks. As he tucked in, I sat down on the floor next to him and removed my Nike trainers.

"Virgil old son, I'm probably going to need your help on this case," I told him. "I know you're only a cat and won't be able to do anything other than listen to me but it will help me just to get everything straight in my head if I can tell you what's been happening, and fill you in on my progress." I stroked Virgil, telling him the whole story. He gazed at me unblinkingly out of his one green eye. He'd lost his other eye in a bitter fight over a fish bone some years before. His opponent—a bad-tempered Doberman—was still seeing a pet psychologist. Virgil and I had been together a long time. I'd gone to the Cats Protection League looking for a cute fluffy kitten and came home with a hard-boiled spitting tomcat with a torn ear and a mean disposition. Story of my life, actually.

An ex-boyfriend of mine who was a Cambridge Professor had been impressed by the fact that I'd named my cat after some ancient Roman poet who had written a poem about some woman called Enid. I didn't have the heart to tell him my cat was actually named after the handsome, if slightly wooden, pilot of Thunderbird 2.

After I finished telling Virgil the events of the morning, he belched tuna at me and sauntered over to my MFI bookcases, his tail twitching. He surveyed the shelves, then jumped up, knocking the figure of Orlando Bloom in the role of Legolas to the floor. Luckily it didn't break—

I'd got it from a Kellogg's Cornflakes packet and the figurine was plastic. I'd had to eat cornflakes before and after every meal for six weeks before I found a Legolas. I had a kitchen drawer stuffed with thirty-eight ugly little plastic figures of orcs and trolls. As I say, story of my life. As I picked up Legolas and placed him reverently back on the shelf, I smiled to myself. It really seemed as though Virgil was looking for a specific book amongst my crime fiction collection. He put out his paw and knocked one of the books to the floor—*The Cat Who Vomited Furballs All Over The Carpet* or something like that.

I left him to his games and went into the kitchen to make myself something to eat. I opened the Electrolux fridge. Things were looking a bit bare in there. I really needed to go shopping. I pulled out a Sainsbury's Gourmet Duck Meal For Two With Asparagus And Cabbage Mash and popped it in the microwave. I didn't like to buy from the Sad And Pathetic Meals For One range. I liked my shopping trolley to say 'Young, Rich, Successful and Sexy' rather than 'Desperate And Gagging For It'. You never knew who you might meet at the supermarket. So I always bought meals for two, just in case. Well, that and the fact that I really liked my grub and there was never enough in the meals for one-person containers. When the timer pinged I pulled out the dish and put it on a tray with a Gibson (two and three quarter ounces of Gordon's Gin, a dash of Martini Extra Dry Vermouth and a small Branston cocktail onion) and took the tray into the living room.

Virgil was sitting on the floor in front of the bookcase where I had left him, glaring at me with his one beady eye. The floor around him was covered in scraps of paper that he had scratched out of the book.

"Shit. Damn it, Virgil, just because you don't like crime-solving cats, there's no need to do that." I slammed my tray down and started to pick up the pieces of paper. By some strange quirk of fate some of the words and letters that Virgil had torn out had fallen in such a way that they actually formed a proper sentence—

do Not trust Banks

"You're absolutely right, Virgil, you clever old thing. Why, only last week I got a statement from the bank that was fifty-six pence out. And what about the time they lost that cheque and I went over my overdraft limit by two pounds fifty-nine and they charged me fifteen quid because of it? I'd take my business elsewhere—apart from the fact that I'd have to give *them* money if I did that. But you're right. I don't trust banks. Now, let me have my lunch in peace, would you?"

After I'd eaten I switched on my Phillips 28" TV and watched some inane home decorating show for half an hour. The things these people managed to do with old Andrex toilet roll tubes and gilt paint was amazing. I looked around the living room of my own small, terraced house. Lawrence Llewellyn Bowen would probably call it 'minimalist and eclectic'. It was a bit like my office, really—bare, shabby and mismatched.

I took my tray back into the kitchen, catching a glimpse of myself in the mirror as I passed. Had I really looked that bad when Owen Banks came into the office? Damn, I needed to smarten up my act, lose a hundred pounds or so, get my hair done, buy a new wardrobe, book myself in for a course of liposuction and some serious plastic surgery. One thing at a time. I combed my mousy brown hair and twisted it into an approximation of a neat, Audrey Hepburn-like French twist. It was the closest I would get to looking like Audrey Hepburn. As it was, I looked as though I had *eaten* Audrey Hepburn. I definitely needed to find my gym membership card. People say that I do resemble a film star, though. Unfortunately, it's Margaret Rutherford.

I looked at my Timex watch again. It was 4 pm—I needed to get out and do some investigating. All this time had passed and we hadn't had a real body. Come to think of it, it had been an absurdly long time since I'd seen any body parts (living or dead). If I left now I would have time to conduct some interviews before meeting Owen Banks in The Royal Flush. Yes, indeed—time to conduct some random interviews with some random bad guys in some random bars in the seediest part of town. It was time to hit Sleazy Street. I wasn't sure what I was going to ask my interviewees, but no doubt inspiration would strike when we got face to face.

I decided to change before heading out. In the office, I'd been wearing Levi jeans, the Nike trainers, a Top Shop t-shirt and a thick Arran sweater from British Home Stores. It was snowing outside and my office was cold. Since I was going to be spending time in bars, I thought I'd better tidy up a bit. I ran upstairs, pulled my white Miss Sixty spandex mini skirt and matching halter neck top out of the wardrobe and lay down on the floor to wriggle into them. Shoes? Well, it could only be the Manolo Blahniks with the five-inch stiletto heels. I couldn't walk more than five steps in them but hopefully I wouldn't have to walk very far this evening. And I definitely wouldn't have to run. I was only going to ask a few bad guys a few random questions. How bothersome could that be?

I was just about to leave the house when the phone rang. I picked up the receiver.

"Ms Handbasket?"

"Yes—who is this?"

"My name is Luke Warmwater—the name won't mean anything to you. Just think of me as a friend who has your health in mind." The voice on the other end of the line was raspy and muffled.

"Oh, that's nice—thank you very much. Actually, I have been feeling a bit bleargh just recently—I think it's that time of the month, you know? So it's nice of you to be concerned. I've been thinking about taking Evening Primrose Oil and getting some Camomile tea—what do you think? Have you tried Camomile tea? And, if we're talking about health, you really ought to go to the doctor about that sore throat of yours."

"What? Look, never mind that. I need to tell you this quickly as I'm afraid they're on their way to kill me right now. As soon as I finish this call and pack a few things, I need to go into hiding. I have some important information for you about Robin Banks."

"Oooooh, lovely. Just hang on a minute while I get a notepad and pen."

"Well, hurry up. They could be here to kill me at any time."

I put the receiver down on the table and went off to hunt for a notepad. I also took a couple of minutes to nip to the loo and get a can of Pepsi out of the Electrolux. I then gave Virgil a vitamin pill, watered the plants and fed them with Baby Bio and topped up my Clinique lipstick. I was back in a matter of seconds.

"Okey dokey—fire away."

"Jeez—that took you long enough. Look, I have all the information you need on the Banks case but I can't tell you over the phone. I need to meet you urgently. Can you meet me tomorrow at 11 am?"

"Hang on, I'll just get my diary." I picked up my diary from the dining room table where it was almost hidden by the day's post. While I was there I was slightly sidetracked by the mail—the telephone bill (had I really spent that much calling Joe's Pizzeria?), a nice long letter from my friend in Guam, and a wedding invitation from an ex-boyfriend. I nipped to the bedroom to see if I had anything to wear to a wedding at which I absolutely definitely had to shine, or whether I needed to go shopping. I wondered what I could wear to upstage the bride—short of an outfit from Pronuptia Bridal Wear, I didn't have a clue. Would it be too much to wear a frothy white dress complete with veil and train to someone else's wedding? I would have to think about that one. I suddenly remembered why I had my diary in my hand and I ran back downstairs and picked up the receiver again.

"Righty-ho, let's have a look . . . No, tomorrow at 11 is out I'm afraid. How about a week on Thursday? I can fit you in before I have my nails done."

There was silence on the other end of the phone.

"Hello? Hello? . . . Hello . . . errrrr . . . Raspy Voiced Friend? Are you still there?"

At the other end, the caller quietly replaced the receiver. Oh well, it was probably only some nutter. I'd forgotten his name, but his call couldn't have been that important. He'd sort of rabbited on about nothing for ten minutes. Although it *was* nice of him to be concerned about my health. Maybe he'd call back some time.

I checked my handbag—mobile phone, pepper spray, lipstick, Uzi. I took the Uzi out and checked the chambery thing. It was fully loaded with twelve hundred bullets. I was ready to go. I said goodbye to Virgil and headed out to question some bad guys.

CHAPTER FOUR

(Takes A Licking But Keeps On Kicking)

I climbed into my car and turned the CD player on. As the strains of Ann Miller's 'Too Darn Hot' gave way to The Cramps 'Can Your Pussy Do The Dog?' I pulled away from the kerb, put the car into second and drove in a northerly direction up Acacia Avenue. After a distance of about fifty yards I hooked a sharp left into Pine Tree Way and drove up the hill. At the T-Junction at the end of the street I turned right into Bamboo Road, getting stuck behind a rusty white van whose driver appeared to be asleep at the wheel. I screeched into fourth gear and overtook White Van Man at seventy miles an hour. I leaned over and rolled down the passenger window so that I could shout 'Wanker' at him as I passed.

I shot through an amber light at the crossroads, turning left into Oak Tree Court. I swore as I realised I'd turned into a cul-de-sac, then swung round and shot through the junction with the lights at amber again, this time making sure I was on Oak Tree Road instead of Oak Tree Court. As bad luck would have it, my inadvertent detour meant that I was now stuck behind the same white van which was still pootering along at ten miles an hour. I screeched into fourth gear and overtook him at seventy miles an hour shouting 'Wanker' at him very loudly as I passed.

At the end of the road, and with the CD player now playing Johnny Cash's 'San Quentin,' I took a left turn onto Eagle Way, slowing down as I neared the bend so that I could look into the window of the new shoe shop that had just opened, and immediately afterwards signalled to turn right into Speckled Thrush Road. Too late I noticed the roadworks at the corner of Speckled Thrush Road and ran over a huge bag of cement. Unfortunately, one of the workmen was carrying the cement at the time and he chased me for about fifty yards but gave up as I turned into Blackbird Avenue. I then turned immediately right into Peacock Street. I took the second exit from the roundabout at the bottom of Peacock Street into Sleazy Street and pulled up at the kerb.

Of course, it wasn't the quickest way of getting to Sleazy Street—if I'd left my house and headed in a southerly direction on Acacia Avenue and driven a hundred yards or so along the road, I would have turned into Sleazy Street from the other end and it would have taken two minutes instead of twenty. But sometimes a girl likes a little drama in her life.

Sleazy Street wasn't a place I would normally choose to come. All the criminals hung out here, as well as some not very nice people. Most of the buildings had been condemned some time ago and rolling tumbleweed would not have been out of place barrelling along the street with the theme tune of 'The Good, The Bad and The Ugly' playing in the background. The term 'urban regeneration' would have been set upon and beaten up if it had dared show its trendy little face. Coffee bars and yuppie restaurants had not found their way down here yet and the warehouses were still warehouses, rather than overpriced flats with a lovely view of the canal. The shops were gradually closing, one by one, and most of the remaining businesses were strip joints, bars, off-licences and video stores. I surveyed the tempting looking bars. Where should I start?

Across the road from where I'd parked was a dive called The Broken Bottle Covered In Blood. People had always told me to steer clear of the place, saying it was the worst bar in town. OK, so it had barbed wire on the windows, graffiti on the walls, piles of vomit in the car park and a neon sign above the door that said 'Keep Out, Nosey Bitches' but really, how bad could it be?

Trying to avoid the worst of the vomit, I tiptoed across the car park, which was really just an empty lot and hesitated for a moment before I opened the door and strode into the bar, carefully stepping over the body at my feet. He might have been dead—the smell certainly made my eyes water, and his stomach was bloated, but that might have been a lifetime of beer and pork scratchings rather than anything more sinister. Although, come to think of it, he could very well have been lying there for about the past thirty years—his t-shirt was advertising the 1974 Reading Rock Festival and his hair was the mullet style so beloved of ELO fans in the 1970s.

As my eyes adjusted to the gloom inside, I noticed that every head in the place had turned (some of them virtually 360 degrees) to look at me. The bar's denizens froze, and a silence descended. The snooker players stood away from the table and stared at me as their balls clicked together (it's strange how often I have that effect on men); the conversations about football, women and shootin' stuff broke off abruptly, and the small, strange-looking boy in the corner stopped playing the banjo and wiped his nose on his dungarees. The place was a Twilight Home for the terminally befuddled. The smartest thing in the place was probably the cockroach fleeing for the exit.

I strolled up to the bar, trying to look nonchalant, as though it hadn't registered that I was the only woman in the place. Oh wait, make that the only woman in the place who hadn't dribbled chewing tobacco down her chest and who had more than one tooth. I felt as out of place as a nun in a brothel. Unthinkingly, I wiped my hand over the stool before I sat down and dirtied my white outfit. My hand stuck to the stool, caught in something worryingly warm and wet. I pulled a face and casually wiped my hand on the sweatshirt of the man standing next to me. As I withdrew my hand and raised it to tuck a stray piece of hair behind my ear, I suddenly realised why that particular article of clothing was called a 'sweat' shirt. I turned to my left and wiped my hand on the coat belonging to the man on the other side. He was collapsed on the bar with his head in his hands, so I thought the chances of him noticing my lapse in manners was slight. My hand came back covered in something that looked as though it had tasted just as bad on the way down. I held my hand away from my side and shook it. I was fast running out of hand cleaning options.

The bartender was drying a glass on a tea towel, which I eyed with envy. However, as he dried, the glass got dirtier, so I decided to give up on the whole hand-cleaning idea and get into the spirit of the thing. The bartender lifted his head so that he could see me from under his beetle brow. "Whaddaya want?"

"I'll have a Cosmopolitan please—two ounces of vodka, a third of an ounce of Cointreau, a third of an ounce of cranberry juice and a third of an ounce of fresh lime juice."

"We ain't got no fresh lime juice."

"No problem. I'll have it without the fresh lime juice."

"We ain't got no freakin' cram berry juice neither lady."

"Just the vodka and Cointreau then."

"Nope. No Quointrew."

"Large vodka. No lemon, no ice."

"We got beer."

"Fine, I'll have a bottle of that then please. No glass."

The bartender took the top off a bottle of Bud with his teeth and slammed it down on the bar, never taking his eyes off me. I felt as though I was being undressed, mentally rolled in batter and deep fried in dirty cooking oil, like a particularly succulent battered sausage.

"That'll be thirty-five quid to you."

I reached into my bag for my purse but a voice said, "Here, let me get that."

I turned. The man who had been asleep on the bar had woken up. He looked as though the bar was his home. His eyes were narrow and close together, his unibrow thick and dark. He was a bad man. I knew that because he had a jail tattoo on his forehead that read: 'Bad Man'. And his faded, ripped t-shirt read: 'Really, Really Bad Man'. He looked like a good candidate for my random questions.

"May I ask you some random questions Mr . . .?"

"Poole. Gene Poole." He held out a hairy mitt, dirt encrusted under the fingernails. It reminded me of Robin Banks. But unlike Robin's, the hand he held out had HATE tattooed on the knuckles of his fingers in blue ink. I sneaked a glance at the other hand. The word HAT was tattooed in black. Since he only had three fingers, I guessed he couldn't fit the E on, but I got the gist of what he was trying to say. "You kin ask, girlie, but you may not like the answers."

"Well, we'll just see how it goes, shall we?" I said brightly, digging my notepad and pen out of my bag. "My first question . . . hmmmmm . . . let's see . . . I know . . . have you ever thought of getting that eyebrow waxed?"

He looked at me. "Get to the point lady. I got some drug deals to see to and some legs to break before the evening's out."

"Oh, well, I won't keep you since your time is obviously so valuable. What do you know about Robin Banks?"

His eyes widened. Well, as far as the simian folds in his brow allowed at any rate.

"What did you say, girlie?" He spoke through gritted teeth—which was no mean feat since he had very few grittable teeth. His breath crawled through the gaps in nauseating waves of unpleasantness. It was as though it couldn't wait to escape the badly ventilated cavern of his mouth. I casually put my hand in front of my nose and tried to breathe through my mouth. I didn't want to appear rude, but . . . really.

"I didn't mean anything untoward by my question. It's just that you look like a man who would know all about Robin Banks."

He hoisted me off the stool by the arm, the stool clattering against the bar as it fell, and dragged me into the corridor by the toilets. Everyone else in the bar who, until that moment had been avidly watching my every move, suddenly decided that anything at all was much more interesting than me. They went back to their drinking, pool playing, sliding into an alcohol induced coma—anything to avoid meeting my eyes. Gene Poole stopped in the corridor, shut the door behind us, and slammed me up against the wall.

"Ow!" I squealed. "That's a little bit sore you know. You obviously aren't aware of your own strength, Mr Poole."

"You'll keep quiet about robbing banks if you know what's good for you, missy." He shook me, pulling my arm out of its socket and dislocating my shoulder. I began to worry that I had picked the wrong random bad guy to ask random questions of. He grabbed me by the neck and lifted me up, hooking me onto the antler of a moth-eaten stuffed stag hanging at an angle on the wall of the corridor. The stag had definitely seen better days, although it looked as though it would be hard-pressed to remember any of them. Fake pine cladding is never a good look and, when accompanied by stuffed road kill, it's an absolute decorating disaster. As I dangled, kicking and screaming, my feet a good six inches above the floor (even taking into account the stiletto heels), Gene Poole punched me in the stomach and chest, several times. I heard ribs crack. Unfortunately, they were mine.

I'd obviously hit a nerve. "I just want you to tell me what you know about Robin Banks. Surely that's not such a big secret is it?"

He pulled a gun out of his jeans pocket and pointed it at me. It was a . . . oooooh . . . now what were those big guns with the wooden handles called? . . . oh yes, a double-barrelled shotgun. He fired at me in anger, missed me and hit the stag's head instead, causing a storm of dust and dirty stuffing. He fired again. I dived out of the way, forgetting that I was attached to an antler, and my white spandex halter-top ripped. The bullet slammed into the wall behind me as I landed on the floor, my left leg crumpling underneath me. He fired again and again as I rolled out of the way backwards and forwards, dodging the bullets, hitting my head on the walls several times in my desperation to avoid the shots, my ribs shooting pains into my chest with every turn.

"God damn it—how many bullets does that thing have?" I shouted.

"Lots!" He fired again just to prove it.

I staggered to my feet, blood sluicing into my eyes and down the front of my wrecked blouse, and he raised his gun and shot at me again. As I ducked, the door to the men's toilet behind me opened and a man stepped out, doing up his flies. The bullet hit him in the middle of the chest and he flew about ten feet backwards through the air in slow motion before coming to rest, face down, in the urinal. I took advantage of the distraction and dived headfirst out of the nearest window, crashing through the glass. I landed on the packed dirt outside the window, dislocating my knee. I checked myself, all over. Luckily, the glass from the window hadn't cut me to ribbons. In fact, I was laceration-free. It was as though the window was made of magic glass, that couldn't pierce through human flesh. What were the chances of that happening, I wondered. It must have been my lucky night.

I thought I'd better take myself off to hospital, anyway, so I dragged myself to the car, trailing my bad leg behind me and holding my dislocated shoulder. The blood was still pouring down my face from my several massive head wounds but as I reached the car I managed to make out a shadowy figure standing by the driver's window with a rock in his hand. Someone was trying to break into my car. Really, this was an unbelievably high crime area. Where were Neighbourhood Watch when you needed them?

"Hey!" I shouted. "What the hell are you doing?"

The figure jumped back from the car and started to run. I chased him down the road for a couple of hundred yards, gaining all the time. I was just about to launch myself at him when I caught the heel of my Manolo Blahnik in one of the potholes that pock-marked Sleazy Street. I made a mental note to call the council offices when I got home. My Council Tax was obviously not being spent on the highways. Or the police. The car thief swerved down a side street and tried to elude me by climbing an eight-foot fence, but I vaulted over it like a gazelle with a dislocated knee and massive head wounds and was now breathing down his neck (although wheezing down his neck was probably more accurate). As we landed in the street at the other side of the fence, the thief rolled out of the way of my hands. We both got up and I was just about to grab hold of him when a truck speeding towards me with its horn blaring and headlights flashing caught my attention. I had to let the thief go as I dived out of the way of the truck and onto the verge at the side of the road. I landed in a steaming pile of something which had been left by either an extremely large dog, or a small cow. Apparently, the good luck which had been scampering after me so far had decided to call it a night.

The truck driver insisted on calling an ambulance even though I told him I was fine and just needed to sleep it off. Sure, I'd feel stiff in the morning, and I'd have a few blisters from where my 5" stiletto shoes had rubbed me, but I'd felt worse after a night out down the disco with the girls, strutting my funky stuff. But the truck driver was so concerned that I decided to humour him, and insisted he come with me as he was obviously suffering from shock and shaking like a leaf. He agreed, on the proviso that he could stand upwind of me so, while we were waiting for the ambulance to arrive, I got into his big rig and drove it to a safer spot just up the road, before jogging back to where the ambulance had just arrived.

At the hospital I lay on the gurney as the doctor poked and prodded at my tender flesh. "So, what's the damage, Doc?"

"Four broken ribs, a fractured jaw, a broken wrist, a dislocated knee, several massive head wounds, two black eyes, you've lost four pints of blood, your kidneys are swollen to the size of basketballs, you have a dislocated shoulder, a bullet wound in the soft fleshy part of your upper arm, a broken arm and a bad head cold. Your cholesterol level is up at seven point two and you could do with losing a hundred pounds or so. You are also covered in dog shit and you smell disgusting—I'm no vet, but that dog has definitely eaten something dodgy. However, the good news is that for a fifty year old, you're not in bad shape."

"But doctor—I'm thirty-five . . ."

"Then you're in big trouble. We'll keep you in for a couple of weeks, run some more tests. See if there's any hope for you."

I looked at my watch. "Sorry, Doc—no can do. It's nine-thirty and I need to meet my client at ten. Just give me some band aids, a damp flannel and a couple of painkillers and I'll be OK."

"I really can't let you do that. I'm sorry, but I won't give my permission for you to leave. You're in a bad way. You need round-the-clock nursing care and a good long bath."

"Then I'll sign myself out."

"Miss Handbasket, I strongly advise against it, but if that's the way you feel, I can't stop you." He handed me a form.

I gave it a cursory read through.

```
I  . . . . . . . (patient's name) realise that I
am as stupid as heck and the lovely doctor knows
better than I do what is good for me. However,
```

I'd like to leave this hellhole now and won't sue
anybody in the morning.
    Love, ... (patient's name)

I signed the form with my good hand and limped out of the hospital.
Time to go and meet Owen Banks in The Royal Flush.

CHAPTER FIVE

(Enter The Strong Arm of The Law)

I jogged back to The Royal Flush, getting there just a couple of minutes before 10 pm.

The Royal Flush was a couple of steps in class above The Broken Bottle. No bars crisscrossed the windows, the graffiti on the walls was spelled correctly (the four letter words at any rate), and sawdust had been spread on the floor to soak up the blood. Inside, the light was dim—only one bulb in every two was working; I wasn't sure if this was due to economy or the owners' attempt to create a romantic atmosphere—but I could see that the clientele were in a different class too. That is to say, most of them looked as though they hadn't fallen out of the same family tree and landed face first on the pavement. It still wasn't The Ritz, but at least I didn't feel as though I was on the set of *Deliverance,* about to squeal like a pig.

Owen Banks was sitting at the bar with a bleached blonde draped all over him like a sleazy, emaciated fur coat. A rat fur coat. Well, okay, she wasn't covered in fur. A bald, rat fur coat. Point is, what was the rat-bitch doing cosying up to my man? He still hadn't changed his clothes, still hadn't washed, and his breath could remove paint from walls at fifty paces but he made parts of me tingle. I'm not sure what those parts were for because I hadn't used them in years, but the tingling felt good.

Owen waved me over. "Hi, Helena. This is my girlfriend, Barbara—Barbara Seville."

Barbara Seville and I nodded coldly at each other, and then I turned back to my man. "Owen, I have some things we need to discuss. In private," I said pointedly.

Barbara Seville oozed off the bar stool like rat vomit with a bad dye job. "Don't worry, honey, I've got better things to do. Owen, big boy, lend me your car will you? I need to see a friend. I'll be back when you two lovebirds have finished your *important* private chat. Oh, and can you lend me your big hooded jacket too—it's really cold out there."

"Sure, angel." Owen passed over his jacket and car keys. Barbara shrugged into the jacket and put the hood up around her little rat face. In the jacket she looked remarkably like Owen—well, apart from the fact that she was two feet shorter and 150 lbs lighter. But . . . in a certain light and if you were really, really drunk, you wouldn't be able to tell them apart.

She flounced out, spitting a piece of advice my way as she exited. "Oh, honey, did nobody ever tell you it was a fashion faux pas to wear white shoes before May Day?"

"Apparently not, *sweetie*. Just as they never told you that a woman with breasts the size of pimples shouldn't wear a blouse slit to her waist. You look like a plucked chicken."

OK, so I wasn't proud of myself for resorting to bandying breast insults with another woman, but at least I'd moved on from the rat analogies. She slammed the door behind her. Owen ordered me a Fluffy Duck (one ounce of Bacardi, one ounce of advocaat, a third of an ounce of fresh cream, and a dash of lemonade—garnished with a strawberry and a sprig of mint) and I hoicked myself onto the bar stool, pulling my skirt down modestly over the bruises and scratches on my legs.

"What the hell happened to you?" asked Owen, touching me gingerly on the bandage wrapped round my head. "You look like Gloria Swanson in *Sunset Boulevard*."

I tried to sound casual, as though being beaten up, shot at and almost hit by a truck all in one night was an everyday occurrence. "Oh, I just got into a little altercation in a bar up the road earlier. No biggie." I could tell he was impressed. "You should see the other guy." Actually, if I saw the other guy, I would run off screaming, but there was no need to tell Owen that. I started to tell Owen what had happened. In my version Poole was tougher, meaner and had more teeth; I was braver, faster and begged less.

As we looked into each other's eyes, I heard the slamming of a car door outside, followed by an engine firing. I was just opening my mouth to embellish still further the legend of my own derring-do when there was an almighty bang and a roar of flame lit up the bar through the front window. An explosion shook the building. After a few seconds of silence, where everyone froze, reminding me of the time when I farted in the lift after a job interview (I didn't get the job—purely coincidental, I'm sure), everyone in the bar rushed to the door and looked out. Owen's car was burning.

He turned to me, the light from the flames of the explosion which killed his girlfriend and trashed his car flickering over his face, bathing it in a warm, cosy glow.

"Oh, my God—do you think that was meant for me? Because of this thing with Robin and the jewels?" I hadn't thought of the possibility, but I nodded. I didn't want my client to think he was one step ahead of me the whole time. He grabbed me. "Do you think they thought she was me, because she was wearing my coat and driving my car?"

"Yep," I said, leading him back to the bar. "Lucky break, huh?" I adjusted my white spandex mini skirt to show another couple of inches of scratched thigh and watched as a huge tear rolled down his face. Perhaps I'd better show a little sympathy. "I'm sorry for your loss."

"Oh, it's OK. You were right—she did have extraordinarily small breasts. I shall miss the car though."

"I *meant* the car." I patted his hand and ordered us another drink.

At that point, the door to the bar slammed open. A squat, slightly overweight man with broad shoulders and rumpled blonde hair stood there. He had 'cop' written all over him. On his hat, on his jacket, and even picked out in gold thread on the cuffs of his trousers—obviously a man who lived for his job and wanted the world to know it. The lowlife scum in the bar decided that now would be a good time to finish their drinks and slither out. Within twenty seconds only Owen, I, and the bartender were left. And even the bartender had his coat on.

The cop strode over. "You Banks?" Owen nodded.

The cop looked at me. "You Handbasket?"

"Me Handbasket. You Tarzan?"

"Don't be lippy, missy. I could make trouble for you. A lot of trouble. You wanna lose your PI licence? Just go ahead and give me some lip, why don't you."

"Sorry to disappoint, but I don't have a PI licence."

Owen turned to me, aghast. "You don't have a PI licence? What was that certificate on your wall then?"

I blushed. "I bought it over the internet for fifty dollars. I'm also an ordained minister for Sister Hepzibah's Church of The Holy Money Making Scam Batman, and I have a degree in Shoe Science from the University of Blahnik. What can I say? There are cracks in my office wall and I couldn't afford wallpaper."

The cop cleared his throat. "Enough of the chitchat, people. I'm Detective Lee. Frank Lee. I've been trying to track the pair of you down all day. Mr Banks, I was round at your house earlier. You weren't there, so I entered the place illegally and whaddaya know, I found a pair of hands with your fingerprints all over them. Well, apart from the tips of the fingers. Those prints belonged to someone else."

"You carried out an illegal search of my house, Detective? Isn't that . . . illegal?"

"Yep. That's me—the loner cop who doesn't give a crap for the rules."

I was beginning to like this man. And it wasn't just the uniform. I could sense a frisson of attraction between us.

"So, detective . . ." I brushed a donut crumb off the shoulder of his uniform. Or it might have been dandruff, I wasn't sure. "What does your wife feel about you breaking into houses illegally?"

"I'm not married, Ms Handbasket."

"Miss," I breathed, lowering my eyelashes demurely.

"Divorced. Four times. And I'm paying the alimony to prove it. It's tough finding a woman who can put up with being the wife of a cop. Sometimes it feels as though you're married to the job. None of my wives could cope with the hours, the worry, the spoiled dinners, the beatings with a rubber hose. No wonder I'm an alcoholic with bad digestion." He grimaced and rubbed his stomach, which bulged over the belt of his trousers and was threatening to burst out of his jacket. I looked from his glowering face to the hulking figure of Owen Banks on the stool next to me, picking idly at a shaving scab on his chin. Things were looking up on the old romantic front. If I played my cards right, I could be the shuttlecock between these two players in the badminton game of love . . . I could be the hypotenuse in this isosceles triangle of desire . . . I could do with throwing out my Harlequin Romance collection when I got home.

As if to prove his bad digestion, Lee belched, and I was taken back to my teenage years, when I fell in love with the hotdog seller at the summer carnival—heady days of stolen kisses, romantic clinches on the Waltzer, and the delicious smell of two-day-old fried onions.

I turned my attention back to Lee. He was saying, "Are these hands anything to do with your brother, Robin? Rumour has it that he managed to steal a small fortune in jewels from Evan Stubezzi a few years ago and that Stubezzi has been on his tail ever since. You think Stubezzi found him?" His shrewd eyes drilled into Owen, but Owen just stared back impassively.

"And as if these unexplained hands of yours weren't enough, Mr

Banks, I have a serial killer on the loose," said Lee. "Of course, he's not a serial killer yet, since we've only found one body, but the signs are there—a handless body dumped in a woodland clearing, a verse from the Bible stuffed in the corpse's mouth and a scarlet-coloured fish sewn into his chest cavity. We've got the victim down the morgue but we don't even know who he is because we can't find his damn hands. Shit, I don't get paid anywhere near enough to do this job." He pulled a pack of indigestion tablets from his pocket and stuffed three into his mouth at once.

An idea struck me. "Detective Lee, do you think that the handless body in the morgue could in any way be linked to the hands that Owen received in the freezer box? I know it's a long shot, but . . ."

Lee snorted, a haze of chalky powder from the indigestion tablets exploding from his mouth. "Absolutely no connection whatsoever. Just leave the detection to me if you wouldn't mind, Miss Handbasket. Despite what you read in those Nancy Drew books of yours, the police are pretty intelligent you know. So don't go sticking that pretty little nose of yours where it doesn't belong, or I'll haul you down to the station before you can say 'interfering busybody'. Got it?"

"You think my nose is pretty?"

Before Detective Lee could answer, his mobile phone rang—the theme tune from Columbo. He flicked it open and stabbed at the buttons, putting it to his ear with a flourish. "Yep. Like hell I will . . . Do it yourself . . . I'm up to my eyeballs in lowlifes . . . Ah, get stuffed . . . Insubordinate? Hell, yes, I'm insubordinate, Chief. I'm a maverick cop—I do things my own way and don't you forget it." He thumbed the off button. "I've got to go. The Chief wants me to bring in some coffee and donuts." He thrust a finger at us, the nail bitten down to the quick. "I'll be back to talk to you both further about this. In the meantime, don't, I repeat, don't, go nosing around in Evan Stubezzi's business. Despite his respectable façade and his charitable works in the community, he's a dangerous gangland figure with more dirty fingers in more pies than there are careless workers with their dirty fingers in pies at The Pie Factory. Mess with him and you'll get more than you bargained for, and I can assure you, you won't like the bargain."

"If he's that bad, why don't the police just arrest him and stick him in jail?" I asked.

Detective Lee scowled. "Stubezzi could fall in a sewage tank and come out smelling of roses. Handbasket, I'm touched by your faith in the honesty and incorruptibility of the good old British bobby. But I can assure you they're not all as pure as the driven snow. Stubezzi has managed to evade the long arm of the law so far by having half the force in his pocket. Sadly, I'm not one of them. And even if I were, my ex-wives would factor all my ill-gotten gains into the alimony payments."

He turned on his heel, strode to the door of the bar and slammed out in the same way he'd slammed in ten minutes earlier.

Owen and I looked at each other in silence for a couple of minutes, as the bar's regular drinkers sleazed back in and carried on where they had left off.

"We've got to get into the morgue and have a look at the handless body, haven't we?" said Owen. I nodded. "But how the hell are we going to do it? They're never going to let us get a look at that body—why should they? You're an unlicensed private eye and I'm a man with two pairs of hands."

Suddenly, I remembered that I had a very good friend who was a palaeontologist—or whatever those people were called who cut up bodies in morgues. I pulled out my mobile, which reminded me that I needed to recharge it, as it had been two months since I last did so. One of these days it would cut out on me at a most inopportune moment, and then I'd be sorry.

I rang the Morgue. It was late, but I was hoping that my friend would still be there. She seemed to like it there at night. In fact, it struck me that I'd only ever seen her at night, never during the day.

"Hello, the Morgue."

"Oh, good evening. I wonder if I could speak to Katya Fallingstar?"

"Helena? Dahlink, how are you?"

"I'm fine thanks, Katya. Listen, do you have a handless body in one of your shiny drawers?"

"Let me look, dahlink." I heard her feet tapping across the tile floor and the sound of big shiny metal drawers being opened.

"I haf an atrophic male missing his auricles," the drawer closed on its runners and I heard another one sliding out, "a brachycephalic woman with bilateral gun-shot wounds," drawers sliding again, "a male with the cortex of his cerebellum destroyed by blunt force trauma with a cricket bat. Ah, and here we are, a handless corpse with a grumpy expression. A nice, fresh body, just recently killed. Like a bread roll just out of a warm oven."

"That'll be him," I said, making a mental note to steer clear of the bread rolls next time Katya invited me round for dinner. In fact, on second thoughts, I made a mental note to plead a previous engagement next time she invited me round for dinner. "Can we come and see him?"

"Of course, dahlink. Open house here, yes? I am just about to perform autopsy on him. You like to come see?"

"Katya, you're an absolute star." I looked at my watch. "We'll be there in just a little while."

"I leave the door open for you. You come downstairs to the basement, and through the large swinging doors. I leave the lovely blue slippers outside. Please put them on. I chust mopped the floor."

I closed my phone and turned to Owen, who had been looking at me throughout the conversation with a puzzled expression.

I beamed at him. "The good news is, we may have found the part of Robin that isn't in a freezer box in your house. The bad news is, he's just about to be sliced open with a powerful electric saw."

CHAPTER SIX

(I Learned Lots Of Medical Stuff For This Book And, By George, I'm Going To Include It)

Owen burst into tears as Katya pulled back the sheet and revealed the body, like a magician unveiling her latest trick. "It's not my brother," he said.

"Are you sure?"

"Of course I'm sure. This man looks nothing like him. I know I haven't seen him for five years, but I'd recognise my own brother. I told you Robin is . . . was . . . forty, six foot four, and weighed 230 pounds. This man is at least sixty years old, five foot two and only about 100 pounds—even if you add back in the weight of his hands."

"A hard life? Atkins? A new identity courtesy of the Witness Protection Programme?"

Owen shook his head. "It's not Robin."

I turned to Katya, who was standing watching us, dressed from head to toe in green scrubs, a matching hairnet pulled rakishly over her ultra-short bleached blonde hair. Her face was devoid of make-up and she had a scalpel tucked behind her left ear. "Do the police have any idea who this man is?" I asked her.

"They are stumped. Completely so."

"Where are his clothes? Did he have any belongings that might provide some clues?"

Katya fetched me a plastic bag from one of the neat metal shelves that lined the sterile white and stainless steel room. "Here you are, dahlink. I don't think you find anythink useful."

I opened the bag and took out the first item—a black sock with a hole in the toe. I folded down the top. There, inside, was a nametag sewn in with neat stitches: Luke Warmwater. Now, where had I heard that name before? I thought for a moment. Nope, it just wasn't coming to me. I pulled out a shirt—blue, with a frayed collar and cuffs and sweat stains under the arms. I gingerly checked the collar with its greyish mark of age and wear, and an indicator of someone who didn't bathe too often. Another nametag with the same name. I reached into the bag and pulled out a surprisingly smart red leather wallet and opened it. £16.56 in notes and coins, various credit cards, library card, video rental card, drivers licence—all with the same name and address. And the clincher: a folded piece of paper in the section of the wallet where a photograph would normally be. I unfolded it and read: 'If this wallet should dare to roam, box its ears and send it home—to Luke Warmwater, Flat 1b, 18 Laurel Court, Wolverham, Essex, England, Europe, The Earth, Near The Moon, The Solar System, The Universe.'

I took out my cell phone and called Detective Lee. He thanked me morosely and told me he'd send a team to Laurel Court right away and that he would call me back and let me know what they found. He also added that, despite his grateful thanks, I was immediately to back off and leave the investigating to the professionals. He made the nose comment again, but this time the word 'pretty' was not mentioned, which I found a little worrying.

I could tell that Owen and Katya were impressed with my sleuthing skills and I basked in their acclaim for a few minutes before saying, "Anyway, no time to waste. We have a body to dissect. Katya, I'm no expert, but it looks as though he's been stabbed twice in the chest causing him to bleed to death, and his hands have been cut off at the wrists. Is that right?"

Katya wrinkled her nose. "It is more difficult than that, dahlink. Pass me the electric saw and the pruning shears and I will let you know once I haf rummaged around in his insides."

She cut a Y-shaped incision in the body of Luke Warmwater. Having done so, she rummaged around as promised and took out a few slithery bits and pieces, which she raised to her cheek, muttering "Hmmm, still warm" to herself. I could tell that she had forgotten we were there, and that she was much more comfortable with the dead than she was with the living. Her body relaxed, and her clipped Eastern European accent thawed out as she muttered to the corpse on the table. She treated the body parts with dignity and care, placing them gently into little metal trays, and weighing them. Every now and then she would cut off small pieces of the organs she removed and put them into jars, writing out labels in a tiny, neat print. As she worked she hummed a medley of Rod Stewart songs, from 'First Cut Is The Deepest' to 'Hot Legs', via 'Do Ya Think I'm Sexy' and 'Every Beat of My Heart.' I gritted my teeth and suffered through it, breathing a sigh of relief as she finished with a flourish. My relief was premature. She was just taking a break.

Within thirty seconds she had launched into 'Sailing', like a battleship full steam ahead. I was ready to bop her over the head and slide her into one of the morgue drawers by this time, but I was too busy trying to breathe through my mouth and keep my dinner down. I could see that Owen was also struggling—whether with the singing or the body parts I wasn't sure—but he'd turned a very pale green and gone for a lie down on one of the tables. An empty one, I'm glad to say.

With a final reassuring pat on the corpse's arm Katya looked up and seemed to recall she had company. She collected all her samples and stuffed them into a large padded envelope. "I took some microbiologic cultures, did a Nitroblue tetrazolium and some tissue sampling for cytogenetics. I send these upstairs for lots of testing. There is toxicology, and a CAT scan oriented brain dissection. Plus liver function tests and tests on the stomach contents." She shook the contents of the largest jar rather too close to my face and I stepped back slightly. Sometimes I thought Katya's social skills were sadly lacking.

She slid the envelope into a wide metal chute that went up into the ceiling—and from there presumably, into the lab above—and pulled the handle. "The results take maybe two, three weeks. The lab peoples are very busy."

"Any chance of getting the results a little quicker?" I asked.

Katya shrugged and picked up the phone, dialling an internal number. "A favour, please, dahlink Lab Boy. Yes, I know you did me favour last week, but they do it on *CSI: Las Vegas* all the time . . . Please hurry my results. Thank you."

Katya put the phone down and smiled at me. "Television has much to answer for. Anyone would think these things can be done straight away. Is just not true."

The metal chute rattled loudly, making Owen and I jump.

Katya removed the envelope that clattered into the tray at the bottom. "Ah, here are results." She opened the envelope and read the sheet inside, nodding occasionally as she did so. "Yes, I discovered two homogenous macroscopic longitudinal excisions in the thorax and into the pericardial mesothelium, which penetrated the epithelium and the epidermis, thus causing exsanguination of the atrium and the anterior vena cava. There was also some tearing of the muscularis mucosae. In addition, the carpi were sliced bilaterally through the dermal stratum corneum."

"So, what does that mean in layman's terms, Katya?"

"He's been stabbed twice in the chest causing him to bleed to death, and his hands have been cut off at the wrists."

I called Detective Lee to give him the results of the autopsy, and also to see what they had found at Laurel Court.

"Well, not that it's any of your business—I told you to keep your nose out of police matters—but, yes, Luke Warmwater's flat was the crime scene. The murder was carried out here and then the body was dumped in the woods where a man out walking his dog found it. Don't ever buy a dog by the way—it increases the chances of your coming across a corpse a thousandfold. Nasty, unlucky bastards dogs are."

"Any possibility that I could nip round tomorrow and have a look?" Maybe seeing Warmwater's flat would ring a bell as to where I knew his name from.

"Sure, no problem, but once you've had a look just butt out and leave it to the professionals. The key's under the mat. If you wouldn't mind treading a bit carefully and look out you don't step in any pools of blood, we'd be grateful. The forensics boys haven't had a chance to nose round the place yet so don't move anything, touch anything, or otherwise interfere with anything." Detective Lee yawned. "I'm going home to bed. It's been a solid thirty-six-hour shift. It's tough being a maverick cop with no partner to share some of the burden. And all I have waiting for me at home is a bottle of Glenfarclas whisky, a cupboard full of pot noodles and my huge collection of Gregorian Chant CDs."

If I hadn't been so tired myself, I would have taken that as an invitation, but before I did so, I needed to find out who Gregorian Chant was. I couldn't recall his name from the Top 40 countdown and wondered if he was one of these infernal Justin Timberlake clones, but Detective Lee didn't look as though he would be a big fan of boy bands.

Owen and I thanked Katya who was scrubbing down the metal tables and the white tiles of the chilly morgue so that it was spick and span and ready for the next corpse. We asked her if she wanted a lift but she declined. "I have much slicing and dicing to do this evening, Helena. I cannot go home until the last sternum is stripped and the last duodenum is dissected. These bodies will not autopse themselves, you know."

We left her to it and exited into the night. Again, the thought crossed my mind that Katya preferred the dead to the living. For some reason, the thought made me a little queasy. Or maybe it was just the lingering aroma of formaldehyde.

Since Owen's car had exploded, I gave him a lift home before heading home myself. If he'd asked me in I would have had to turn him down, since I was so tired. However, I felt unaccountably let down that he didn't ask, just mumbled a distracted goodbye and went into his house without a backwards glance. I drove home and parked at the kerb. Inside, I collapsed onto the sofa. I kicked my shoes off and rubbed my feet, groaning. My leg was aching where I had dislocated the knee earlier, and I had a hell of a headache but otherwise there were no ill effects from the evening's excitement. A couple of aspirin and a long lie the next morning would do me the world of good.

Virgil meowed and I turned my head. He was sitting on the chair in front of my laptop, which I had left switched on. I had left in a hurry earlier and forgotten to close down.

"What is it, old son? Have you been playing solitaire while you've been waiting for me?" I laughed to myself and went over to the desk, carrying my shoes in my hand. Virgil nudged the screen with his head. There was a Word document on screen and I glanced at it quickly, leaning over to switch the computer off.

```
robin banks is not to be trusted katya
fallingstar is afraid of daylight and garlic
and gregorian chants are a type of early
english liturgical music named after pope
gregory i by the way theres a message on
your answering machine from a strange man who
sounded as though he was speaking through a
handkerchief asking you to meet him in the
woods at 2 AM don't go
```

How odd. Who on earth had written this unpunctuated nonsense—it was practically incomprehensible? I scooted Virgil off the chair and sat down to have a closer look at the screen, but unfortunately I dropped one of my shoes onto the keyboard. The document disappeared. Damn. What had it said again? All I remembered was that Gregorian Chants were named after a Pope. Damn, damn, damn. I wish I'd read it more closely. Besides, if someone had taken the time and trouble to break into my house and leave a message on my computer, then they could have left me something useful instead of musical trivia.

I went into the kitchen to get myself a drink. Some vitamin C would help clear my head. As I mixed myself a Fuzzy Navel (one ounce of vodka, one ounce of peach schnapps, five and a half ounces of orange juice, garnished with a slice of orange and a maraschino cherry) I noticed that the message light was flashing on the answering machine.

There were two messages.

One was from Fifi. "Helena, doll, two cackle-broads came in to see you earlier—slinky pieces of homework—friends of Robin Banks with some jingle-brained tale of dipsy doodle. We bumped gums for a while but the twists ankled like shit through a tin horn when they found out you were with the elephant ears."

I contemplated the message for a while but without the aid of a Fifi-to-English dictionary I could only translate about one in ten words. I think that the general gist was that two rather hoity-toity but good-looking women had popped in to see me, professing to be friends of Robin Banks and telling a bizarre tale of chicanery. Fifi had chatted to them for a while but they'd apparently left rather swiftly when Fifi had told them I was assisting the police with their enquiries. But that was a wild guess.

The second message was from a strange man who sounded as though he was speaking through a handkerchief, asking me to meet him in the woods at 2 am.

"Come alone, don't tell anyone you're coming, and leave all your weapons at home." The voice was strangely familiar but I couldn't quite put a finger on it. Oh well, I was sure it would come back to me at some point. I finished my Fuzzy Navel and went upstairs to the bedroom where I changed out of my white spandex outfit, which was by now a little the worse for wear, deciding on a pale beige skirt suit, which I thought was more suitable for the woods. The skirt was a little tight. Had it shrunk in the wash? I certainly couldn't be putting on weight when I hadn't been shopping for so long and hadn't a bite to eat in the fridge. I didn't think the Manolo Blahniks would go with the beige suit, so I dug a pair of brown suede kitten-heeled mules out of the wardrobe. I ran back down to the kitchen, thinking I'd better have a snack before going out. I pulled out a tub of Ben & Jerry's Cherry Garcia ice cream and a chocolate éclair. I ate the ice cream straight out of the tub and put the éclair in my handbag for later. Now, let's see, if I was going into the woods I would also need mosquito spray and possibly a pair of socks, just in case my feet got cold in the mules. I put the spray and socks into my handbag with the éclair. My bag was full and wouldn't close with all the extra stuff so I removed my phone, gun and torch and left them on the kitchen counter. After all, I wouldn't be needing those.

CHAPTER SEVEN

(If You Go Down To The Woods Tonight...)

Before I left the house, I wondered whether I ought to ring anyone and let them know where I was going, but then I remembered that the mysterious voice on my answering machine had specifically told me not to tell anyone, so I decided not to. Besides, who would be interested in my nocturnal wanderings?

The woods were fairly near my house so I didn't take the car. I strolled along the path to the end of the road and then cut along the dirt road that led to the allotments. Usually, the allotments were a hive of activity, with mostly elderly men out in all weathers cultivating their neat vegetable patches, or sitting outside their little sheds drinking tea in companionable silence. I liked chatting to the gardeners. I could never manage to grow anything myself, but I relished the peace and quiet, and loved the way all the sheds were painted in different colours and in different stages of disrepair. Tonight the sheds were a uniform silvery dark grey in the moonlight. Had I seen anyone digging, I would have turned tail and run.

As I climbed the slope that led to the woods, the only sound I could hear was my own heavy breathing. Well, the slope was really steep, you know. And I did have a sore knee and various other injuries that slowed me down a bit. The wind was up and the thick clouds were skittering in front of the moon, so from time to time it was as though someone had laid a thick blanket over the whole area. I was beginning to wish I'd brought a blanket with me, or at least a thick jacket. I tugged my little suit jacket closer around me and shivered. I tripped over a root. Why hadn't I brought a torch with me? Whoever would have thought I'd need a torch in the woods after midnight? It also crossed my mind that maybe the kitten-heeled mules probably weren't the best choice for the terrain—even though they went really well with the beige skirt suit.

As I went deeper and deeper into the woods, I realised that I didn't know where I was headed. The message had told me to meet the caller in the woods, but hadn't specified a particular place. Since the woods were about 5 miles square (or 5 miles wood-shaped would probably be more precise) I was just going to have to wander around aimlessly and hope it wouldn't be too long before I stumbled on something.

I immediately stumbled on something. Unfortunately, it wasn't the rendezvous point with my midnight caller, just a large, moss-covered log. I fell over it, twisting my already sore leg, scraping my face on the mossy bark, and tearing a button off my jacket. I reached into my handbag and pulled out the sewing kit I'd picked up in a hotel in Leeds a few months ago, and sat down on the log to do an emergency repair. Luckily, the kit included a selection of different coloured threads— black, white, pink, pale blue and cream. It was difficult to be sure of the colour of thread in the darkness, but I eventually picked out what I thought was the cream, threaded the needle by touch and sewed the button back onto my jacket. The cream thread would match my suit rather well, so I continued on my way, knowing that I was still nicely co-ordinated.

Deeper into the woods, the trees became thicker, extinguishing the light from the moon. The atmosphere around me began to weigh heavy. The pleasant sounds of bunny rabbits at play, the flapping of butterfly wings, and little deer scampering, gradually faded behind me. My pleasant evening walk had turned from *Bambi* to *Blair Witch*. All I could hear was my own breath, the slapping of my mules against my bare heels, the greedy guzzling of mosquitoes as they sucked at my tender flesh and some horrid slithering things that I'd rather not dwell on too much. Oh, and the slow, measured footsteps that had been following me for about ten minutes now, of course. I stopped for a minute or so to get my bearings. I wished I'd brought my compass and a GPS tracking system, a loaf of stale bread to leave a trail of breadcrumbs, and a Forest Ranger, with a blanket and a bottle of champagne. The latter was just pure fantasy.

The footsteps behind me continued to approach for about ten seconds before stopping. I could practically hear the rasp of breath on my neck. Which was a strange experience, because I didn't think I'd ever felt a sound before. Was it the raspy voiced stranger from the earlier phone call? And which raspy voiced stranger in particular? My life was full of strange men with throat infections. I could smell the distinctive aroma of menthol and honey and lemon Throaties, so perhaps whoever it was had taken my advice. I was rather pleased.

The path, which had been getting narrower and narrower and gradually less well trod, suddenly stopped altogether. As I fought my way through nettles, vines and branches, I began to wish that I'd brought my machete. I was, however, very glad that I wasn't wearing nylons and that my legs were bare, as the thorns attached themselves to me, gouging pieces out of my calves and drawing blood. Imagine what they would have done to a pair of 10 deniers.

Instead of fruitlessly wishing I'd brought useful stuff, I soon began to wish that I hadn't come out at all, but tucked myself up in bed with a good book. The latest Patricia Cornwell was waiting for me on my bedside table. I'd left Kay Scarpetta wearing her scuba diving gear and up to her elbows in stomach contents. Or was it a cordon bleu pasta dish? I couldn't recall. Very soon the barrier of branches gave way to a large clearing and a brackish, foul-smelling pond. I skirted around the side of it, determined not to fall into the cold, dirty and unwelcoming water, which looked full of slimy things, some of which I could see, some of which I could only imagine—and those were ten thousand times worse than the slimy things I could see. The moon penetrated weakly through the canopy of trees and cloud cover. As I tried to make out where I was, a large black shape loomed beside me, raised an arm and hit me over the head with something, and, as I stumbled, hit me again.

It felt as though someone was playing the bongos inside my skull. I grabbed the arm and tried to wrestle the blunt instrument from my attacker but he or she brought it down onto my good arm with a crack. I wasn't sure if the crack was my radius or my ulna, but a sharp pain knifed up my arm and rested in my shoulder. I yelled out and dropped to the ground, getting in a kick as I fell. My pointy-toed mule connected with something soft and dangly. He or she was, apparently, a he and it struck me that this was far too cold a night to be out in the woods wearing only your underwear, as this man appeared to be. I heard a grunt of pain and he hesitated temporarily, cupping his groin in that protective way men have, making high-pitched squealing sounds. I hoped the damage was permanent. Somebody who hit defenceless women over the head several times with something heavy didn't ever deserve to have children. The delay gave me time to spring back off the ground, spin round in the air and land a blow to the side of his head with my foot. Unfortunately, I misjudged the spin and he caught my ankle, twisting it until I heard an unhealthy snapping sound. As

I fell back, the dark figure swung his weapon again and it connected with the side of my head, fracturing my jaw for the second time that night. I took a few tottering steps backwards and fell with a splash into the pond. I had a brief, unwelcome thought of slimy things and then everything went black.

XₒXₒXₒXₒX

When I finally came round, dawn was breaking and the clearing was grey and misty. I was lying at the edge of the pond with only my head out of the water. I was colder than a day-old corpse in one of Katya's shiny drawers and I couldn't feel my extremities. I wiggled the fingers of both hands, hoping to get some of the feeling back into them. My right hand stroked my chin. Hang on, where had that beard come from? Had I been out for the count that long? I turned my head and looked at my right hand. My arm was draped over the body of a well-built blue-eyed blonde man lying next to me, and my hand was resting gently on his bearded face. Under normal circumstances, I would have considered this officially 'A Result', but circumstances were decidedly not normal. The blue eyes were glazed and staring, he had deep stab wounds to his chest and his arms stopped abruptly at the wrists. I was cuddling a dead man. Story of my life.

I shrieked and crawled away from the body. It was then that I noticed the hole carved in his chest cavity. A small scarlet fish, also dead, also with glazed and staring eyes, also with no hands, lay in the hole. The only difference between the man and the fish (apart from the beard of course), was that the man had a piece of paper stuffed in his mouth.

I gingerly reached over, plucked the piece of paper out of his mouth and unfolded it. Written on it was a verse from the Bible: "Thou shalt not commit adultery." So, it looked as though the serial killer had struck again, and, if I wasn't much mistaken, he had chosen the Ten Commandments as his theme. A little unoriginal perhaps, but it worked. Assuming he was planning on stopping at ten.

I began to wish I had brought my phone with me. I was tired and sore and it would take me an age to get out of the woods and raise the alarm so I decided that I would build a fire in the clearing and try to signal to the outside world using the smoke from the fire. I had been thrown out of the Girl Guides when I was thirteen, but not before I had attained my 'Semaphore and Smoke Signals' badge. And my mother said it would never come in handy. Hah.

I took my cigarettes and Zippo lighter engraved with the word 'Vixen' out of my handbag. I was trying to give up, but this was not the day. Everything was a little damp from being immersed in the pond, but I finally managed to light one of the cigarettes and took a long draw to calm my nerves. I then set about making a fire in the clearing. It was probably illegal to build unauthorised fires and, with my recent luck, a Forest Ranger would arrest me. But I would cross that bridge if and when I came to it. In fact, I was rather looking forward to it.

I gathered some twigs and leaves, and pieces of bark and things from around the dead man that I hoped weren't clues. The kindling took a while to light due to the dampness as much as my shaking hands, but luckily, the pile of tinder I had accumulated was so damp that the smoke from my fire was thick and strong. I took off my jacket and waved it above the smoke, spelling out my message:

Send help. Dead body. No hands.

I repeated it several times and then dragged over a log from the side of the clearing, and sat down, trying to warm myself in front of the meagre fire. I reached into my handbag and pulled out the chocolate éclair. It was rather soggy and the taste was not enhanced by being soaked in water that fish had widdled in, but I was starving and gulped it down as though I hadn't seen food for days, instead of just a few hours.

I looked down at myself. One of my mules was missing and the other would never be the same again; my beige suit was wrinkled and torn and there was a deep gash in my leg. I took out my invaluable sewing kit. The pink thread wouldn't be a precise match to the colour of the skin on my leg, but it would do until I could get to the hospital. I had just finished sewing up the gash, hoping that I hadn't picked the pale blue thread instead of the pink in the misty dawn light—thus sewing my leg with what would look like blanket-stitched varicose veins—when I heard something crashing through the undergrowth.

Detective Frank Lee appeared in the clearing, red-faced and out of breath, followed by several other policemen and a couple of dogs.

"I thought it must be you, you damn interfering amateur. What the hell are you doing here? And what was that smoke signal message all about? Are you taking the piss?"

"In answer to your very rude and peremptory questions, I am not an amateur. I'm a professional private investigator. And there's no need to snort at that. As for the interfering part. Well, interfering is in the eye of the beholder. What were the rest of your questions? Ah, yes. What I am doing here is 'your job'. The smoke signal message was to get you here quickly. And no, I am not taking the piss. Why would you say that?"

"We've had multiple reports of householders seeing a message in the sky, written in smoke. Our consultant smoke signal expert says the message reads: I've got a lovely bunch of coconuts. Are you not aware of the laws pertaining to campfires in these woods?"

"Well, yes, but I . . ."

He interrupted me: "And here I am on a wild idiot chase, when I have better things to do, like find serial killers."

"And that's what . . ." I gestured to the body on the ground, but he was away ranting again.

"We've wasted manpower and dog power and all because you wanted to have a nice picnic. You still have chocolate and cream on your nose. I can only deduce that you've been stuffing your face with chocolate éclairs."

"Will you please . . ."

"Christ. I should arrest you for wasting police time, setting fires and endangering life and . . ." he tailed off as he finally noticed the body of the handless man ". . . having sex in a public place."

"He's dead, you arsehole!" I yelled at the top of my lungs, determined to get a word in edgeways.

"Then we'll add murder to your list of crimes," Lee bellowed, bringing his face up close to mine in a choleric rage. "And don't call me an arsehole, otherwise 'calling a police officer names' will be on the charge sheet too."

"That's not a real fucking crime, you dickhead. And I didn't kill him. I just woke up, and there he was, dead." I burst into tears of frustration and anger.

"No wonder. He probably stabbed himself and ripped his own hands off after spending a night with you, you harridan." We were both screaming at each other now and the audience of policemen and dogs were looking at us in horrified amusement. Although the dogs might just have been hungry. It's hard to tell with dogs.

"Listen Lee, I'm the sodding victim here. Well, OK, the dead man is too. But I've been accosted by a semi-naked madman (and I didn't even enjoy it), beaten, had my jaw broken, my ankle snapped, my arm fractured, left to drown in a freezing cold pond, and I've eaten nothing but a soggy éclair in the last seven hours. I think I have every right to be a bit pissed off, don't you?"

By the end of this speech my voice had gradually quietened and I contented myself with sobbing gently.

Lee was surveying the dead body. "Christ. It's the same M.O. The only thing that's missing is the Bible verse stuffed in his mouth."

"Oh," I said quietly, teasing the piece of paper out of my pocket. "Here."

Lee glared at me. "If I wasn't already going to arrest you for being a serial killer, I'd arrest you for disturbing the scene of a crime."

"What? You can't arrest me for being a serial killer! I don't fit the traditional pattern, for one thing. Am I a white male between the ages of 20 and 55? For another thing . . . I didn't do it."

Lee pulled out his handcuffs and dragged my hands behind my back. Under different circumstances I might have enjoyed the experience, but on this occasion I was too angry.

"I want my lawyer."

"We'll get him for you when we get back to the nick. Who is it?"

"Well, I don't actually have a lawyer, it's just what everyone says on *The Bill*, so I thought I'd say it."

Lee took my arm roughly.

I yelped. "Watch it—that arm's broken."

He dropped it like a hot potato and grabbed the other one.

"Shit! That one's broken too, you know."

He swore under his breath and dragged me off towards the path, spitting out instructions to his colleagues to call the pathologist and then get the body down to the morgue and comb the clearing for clues, instead of milling around like grannies at a bus stop. I thought now was not the best time to mention that I might have destroyed some of the clues with my fire, since that had seemed to be a sore point. I stumbled after him as best I could but since I had only one shoe and a possible broken ankle, progress was slow. So slow that Lee ended up hoisting me over his shoulder like a sack of coal and striding off along the path. I was impressed. I filed away the strong muscular back for future reference.

CHAPTER EIGHT

(Let's Call In The Experts)

Back at the police station, I was booked, signed in, my belongings were taken from me, and I was given an unattractive white all-in-one suit that made me look like the Michelin Man on a particularly bloated day when he hadn't taken his water tablets. I was thrown into a small cell that reeked of bleach and urine. The walls were a pale, institutional green, the mattress was thin and covered in stains that formed a map of the world in more different types of bodily fluid than I knew existed, and the facilities . . . well . . . I didn't want to write home about them, but if I had then I would have had nothing to say. I wondered why I couldn't have a toilet seat. What did they think I was going to do with it—sharpen the edges and use it as a deadly Frisbee?

After surveying my badly decorated home and finding it wanting, I looked out of the tiny window in the door and banged my fist against the metal.

"Hey," I shouted, "what about my one phone call? I know my rights."

Detective Lee opened the door, brought in a phone and leaned up against the wall as I made my call.

I punched in the familiar number, glaring at Lee all the time. He grinned at me, his arms crossed against his chest, his stomach straining against his creased shirt.

I breathed a huge sigh of relief as the phone was answered after just a couple of rings. "Oh, thank God you're there. I would have been frantic if you hadn't come in yet. I'll have a 12" pepperoni, extra olives, Joe. Could you deliver it to the police station? Cell number . . .?" I looked at Lee.

"Five."

"Cell number five, Joe. A Detective Frank Lee will pay on delivery."

Lee led me to an interview room on the next floor up. B&Q had obviously offloaded their least popular paint shades on the gullible interior police station decorators. The cat-vomit yellow walls clashed hideously with the three bright orange plastic chairs. The only other furniture in the room was a shabby grey Formica table with a tape recorder on it, and a flipchart in the corner, which seemed oddly out of place.

A young policeman entered the room. He looked as though he was just out of school and his mother had bought him a uniform that he would grow into in about ten years time. His skinny neck poked out of his too-wide shirt collar and as he looked at me his face turned a fiery red and his Adam's apple bobbed up and down. I was fascinated by it. But I wasn't sure that he was cut out to be a policeman. If a slightly overweight woman in a white paper suit made him that nervous, what would he do if faced with a gang of bank robbers carrying sawn-off shotguns? Nervously phone his Mum and ask what to do? He was carrying three plastic cups full of a greyish liquid that he assured us was tea. I ignored the strange colour and took a sip. It tasted as bad as it looked. And it looked bad. The young policeman backed nervously out of the room, staring at me as he went. I wiggled my fingers at him in a wave, the paper suit rustling as I did so. His face became even redder and he closed the door behind him with a whimper. I was definitely taking this outfit home.

Lee switched the tape recorder on and did the introductions. As well as the two of us, Lee introduced another CID cop, Chief Inspector Angus Beef. Beef was a small, wiry man with a nervous habit of pushing non-existent glasses up his nose.

"Interview with suspect, Helena Handbasket, commencing at . . ." Lee looked at his watch, " . . . 7.45am." He sat down and nodded at his superior.

"Miss Handbasket," said Chief Inspector Beef in a strong Glaswegian accent. "Can ye tell us whit ye were doing at 3 am?"

"Is that the time of death, Chief Inspector?"

"Aye, missy."

"Well, I was lying in a pond, out cold, having been walloped over the head by some sort of blunt instrument while someone killed a man right next to me, chopped off his hands, carved a hole in his chest and disappeared into the night. How do you like them apples, Chief Inspector?"

Chief Inspector Beef rubbed his nose and tutted. "Well, why did ye no tell us before now that ye had an alibi? Frank, ah think we can dispense wi' the questioning and just get Miss Handbasket tae assist us wi' oor enquiries."

Lee sighed heavily, sat down and opened a file. "If you think so, guv, but I have to say I'm not happy about it."

Angus Beef ignored him. "Now Helena, first things first. We need a really catchy name for the killer and we huv'nae been able tae come up wi' wan. Any ideas?"

I leaned back in my seat. "Let's see. Something alliterative would be nice . . . how about The Bible Basher?" Beef screwed up his face. "No? The Commandment Killer? The Stabber? The Handyman?"

"Och, ah've got it. We'll call him The Murderous, Hand-Stealing, Fish-Leaving Killer."

Lee groaned. "Jeez, guv. It doesn't exactly roll off the tongue, does it?"

"Stop wi' the insubordination, Frank. Now, tell Helena aboot our latest victim. See if she can gie us any help."

Lee read from the file. "The man you were cuddling up to so chummily in the woods was called Justin Case. An accountant, age 47, wife, no children. His wife, Charity, reported him missing this morning when she got up at 6.30. She thought, and I quote, 'he was with that damn floozy of his'. Apparently, Mr Case had been having an affair with his secretary, a Miss Emma Roids."

"Ah," I said, brilliantly, "so he was, indeed, an adulterer, as the Commandment stuffed in his mouth hinted at. What about the first victim—I take it there was a Commandment stuffed in his mouth too?"

Angus Beef slammed his meaty fist on the table. "My God, hen, ye're absolutely right! That's the key to the whole case, right there! There was a piece o' paper in Luke Warmwater's mouth which said 'Thou Shalt Have No Other Gods Beside Me' and his house was covered wi' posters of David Beckham. Personally, ah cannae stand the wee English shite wi' his poncey haircuts, but ye know whit these English pricks are like. Shite—we need tae catch this madman before he kills again. He's still got eight more Commandments tae go."

"Or possibly seven," I said. "Remember, Robin Banks is missing, but his hands have turned up. Oh dear, I do wish I could remember where I had heard the name Luke Warmwater before."

Chief Inspector Beef pulled his mobile out of his pocket. "Frank, ah think we need tae call in the experts on this wan. It's time tae gie the Feebies a bell."

"The who?" I asked.

"The Feebs, EffaBeeEye, The Men In Black."

"The FBI? But . . . aren't they American? Do they have jurisdiction over here?"

Lee slammed his plastic cup down on the table, sending globs of grey tea rolling over the uneven surface like mercury. "Shit, guv, what do you want to bring them in for? They'll just take over and impede our investigation at every turn and then take the credit when we eventually catch the killer."

Beef held up his hand and spoke into the phone. "Hello? Quantico? Can ye spare wan o' your lads? They wans wi' the sunglasses and the sharp suits? . . . Aye, quick as ye like. Thanks, pal." He slipped the phone back into the pocket of his hairy tweed jacket. "He'll be here as soon as possible. They're sending the best they've got—an expert on serial killers, wi' plenty o' experience, fast instincts, brain like a computer. We're in good hands now."

There was a knock on the interview room door. My young admirer who had brought in the teas earlier put his head round the door. He swallowed visibly as his eyes rested on me, and I crossed my paper-clad legs in what would have been an attractive move, had the suit not ripped at the thigh. The policeman looked away and squeaked, "Guv, bloke here to see you." He opened the door wider and a man strode in, taking in the scene at a glance—although how he could have seen much wearing those dark sunglasses I wasn't quite sure. He bumped into a chair and removed the glasses, tucking them into the unzipped breast pocket of his dark Armani suit. He looked at each of the three of us in turn, sizing us up, making an instant decision as to who each of us was. I could see the microchips whirring behind those cool grey eyes, sorting us out like mental reference cards and slotting us away in his brain—the maverick cop who would argue with him at every turn, the disillusioned Chief Inspector biding his time until retirement and, h-e-l-l-l-o, the gorgeous if slightly bedraggled mousy-brown haired PI/ex-murder suspect (OK, so maybe that wasn't what was written on the mental reference card with my name on it, but a girl can always dream). Frank Lee was red-faced and muttering angrily as the stranger moved towards us.

"Good day, y'all. Special Agent Art Ifarti at your service. Chief Inspector Angus Beef, I presume?" he said in a soft accent hailing from the deep south of America. He held out his hand to me. I shook my head.

"Actually, no. I'm Helena Handbasket. That's the Chief Inspector." As he turned to shake Beef's hand, Frank Lee and I looked at each other incredulously. Mind like a computer? Yeah, sure. Maybe a Sinclair ZX Spectrum. A dimwit, but a very handsome dimwit. And that accent was as juicy as an overripe Georgia peach.

I tapped him on the shoulder. "Agent Ifarti, what does your wife think about you having to come all the way over to Britain on a case which might be dangerous and where you might be tempted by a beautiful British woman? Or even an ugly British woman?"

He looked at me with those drop-dead gorgeous eyes. "I'm not married, ma'am."

Things were looking up. I just wished I wasn't wearing the Pillsbury Dough Man's cast-off outfit, and could get my beige suit back.

Agent Art Ifarti rubbed his hands. "So, let's get started, cousins. Whaddaya have?"

Lee remained resolutely silent. From the glances they levelled at each other, it was obvious that my two suitors were not going to get on. I hoped it was sexual jealousy, but it was probably more professional jealousy. It was left to Angus Beef to fill Special Agent Ifarti in.

Beef detailed the two murders to date—the victims, the stabbings, the locations, the scarlet fish in the chest cavity, the biblical tie in, the lack of hands—and also made reference to the missing Robin Banks, but his non-missing hands. "Tae summarise, pal. We've got two dead bodies with nae hands and wan pair o' hands which disnae belong tae either o' the dead bodies."

The FBI man perched on the table with his left buttock (round and peach-like for anyone who's interested), put his right hand on his chin and listened carefully, nodding occasionally.

"A textbook case," he said, when Beef had finished.

Frank Lee sneered. "I suppose you can already tell us everything about the killer then?"

Ifarti gazed at him coolly. "Sure. Everything except his name and address. I'd better leave some little job for *you* to do." Lee bristled and looked ready to square up to him but Ifarti got up and went over to the flip chart, picking up the thick black felt pen on the ledge. "What y'all got here is a white male between the ages of 20 and 55 . . ."

"Oh, well, that narrows it down. Thanks a lot. Quick, guv, let's get the boys to arrest all white males between 20 and 55 and bring them in for questioning. This is a load of crap. I'm not working with this guy." Lee stood, balled up his empty plastic cup and threw it into the corner of the room.

"If all y'all would let me finish . . . as I was saying, y'all's killer is a white male between 20 and 55, of slightly higher than average IQ, working as a labourer." Ifarti thought a moment. "He's a plumber's apprentice . . . yeah, that's it—a plumber. He was bullied at school, his father left the family when the killer was ten years old and the boy regularly wet his bed well into his teens. He tore the legs off spiders and was unkind to neighbourhood pets. He set fires, and was possibly arrested for arson at some point, maybe when he set fire to his school. He lives within a three-mile radius of the crimes in a small terraced house, either on his own or with a female relative . . . an aunt . . ." he pronounced it 'ant' which confused me for a moment, since I couldn't imagine why anyone would voluntarily live with a biting insect. "Yeah, it's his aunt. Her name's Sally. He keeps the hands of his victims in his bedroom, listens to heavy metal music really loudly—he likes Whitesnake, Iron Maiden, Led Zeppelin and Deep Purple. Drives a small red Fiat Uno with a hole in the exhaust. He refuses to wear anything but the colour turquoise. He cuts the heads off flowers, has a complete lack of body hair, walks with a limp, emits a strange odour and eats a lot of cheese."

Apart from the tearing the legs off spiders bit, and the cheese part, the man sounded like a nasty piece of work. He also sounded strangely familiar, but I couldn't quite place him. No doubt it would come back to me at some point.

"What a crock of shit." Lee told me it was time for me to go. I stood up reluctantly. "Don't let this asshole's crap give you ideas, Handbasket. Keep your nose out of my investigation and get back to tailing errant husbands." He put his hand on my shoulder and shoved me out of the room, turning to Angus Beef as he did so. "And you'd better keep this charlatan away from me, guv. I'm a loner, maverick cop and don't work with anyone, least of all Mystic Meg here."

"But I . . ." I tried to get back into the interview room so that I could give Art Ifarti my phone number just in case he needed any more help from me, but Lee propelled me along the corridor, back into the booking room where he shoved my bag of belongings at me and practically threw me out of the police station before storming back inside.

"Don't I even get a lift home, you bastard?" I shouted. "And what about my pizza?"

I set off home, still wearing the ugly white all-in-one paper suit, now complete with rip in the thigh. As a freebie, it didn't make up for the brutality I had suffered at the hands of the police. My leg and ankle were aching a little, and a ten-mile jog home didn't really help, so by the time I got home I was hopping mad—literally as well as figuratively. As I neared the house, I could hear the strains of Led Zeppelin's 'Stairway To Heaven' rattling the windows of the house next door. My neighbour, Jerry Mander, was standing in the garden wearing a turquoise shell suit, slicing the heads off roses with a scythe and munching on a large piece of cheddar.

He looked up as I approached. "Wow, nice outfit, Helena. It really suits you."

"Hi, Jerry." I waved to him as I opened my gate and he raised his strangely hairless hand in response. "This old thing? Oh, it's just something I threw on down the police station when they took my clothes away for questioning." I didn't like to get too close, as Jerry always smelled really weird, but I approached the hedge so that I could hear him over the loud heavy metal music. "You not working at that plumbing job of yours today?"

He limped over to the hedge, shaking his head. "Not today, my car's in for service. It's got a huge hole in the exhaust."

I should have noticed that his little red Fiat Uno wasn't parked in its usual place at the kerb. "So what are you going to do today to keep yourself busy?" I asked.

"Oh, you know," he shrugged, "prune the roses, eat some cheese . . . oh, and I need to clear up that dead spider and its legs from the bathroom."

"Well, have a nice day. And say hi to your Aunt Sally for me, won't you?" I could tell he wanted to say something more, but he just stood there tongue-tied, staring down the front of the white paper suit which was tearing over the chest area, so I waved cheerily to him again as I walked away from the hedge and let myself into the house.

Somewhere in the back of my mind was the key that would unlock this whole case. Unfortunately, it was just like the key to the handcuffs that one of my ex-boyfriends and I had experimented with: lost. I just hoped that when I found the key to the case, it wouldn't be too late. In fact, I hoped that I would find it eventually, and not have to call the fire brigade like we did with the handcuffs scenario. I still shudder and cover my private parts when I hear a fire engine. Funnily enough, the local firemen still shudder and cover their private parts when they see me. A strange sort of symmetry, I guess you'd call it.

Chapter Nine

(Piling On The Suspects)

Entering my house, I was overcome by a sudden wave of fatigue. I felt as though I hadn't slept in over 24 hours. Actually, come to think of it, I *hadn't* slept in over 24 hours. This time yesterday morning I had been sitting in my office wondering whether the PI game was really for me, or whether I should go back to Chiropody College and, since then, I had been beaten up, nearly hit by a truck, had my car broken into, been hospitalised, wrecked two perfectly good pairs of shoes, torn my white halter neck top, been beaten up again, arrested, and come into close contact with two and a half corpses. On top of that I hadn't slept. Unless you counted several hours, concussed, in the arms of a dead man. Personally, I preferred not to count them. It was just like my one and only Club 18-30 holiday to Faliraki, only without the sunburn.

On the plus side, I had met three single, good-looking men. Every cloud has a silver lining. I collapsed onto the sofa and considered my next move. First of all, a hot shower and a strong cup of tea. That should stop the aches and pains and halt the massive internal bleeding. I also needed to get something to eat—yet another day without a trip to the supermarket. I would just have to rustle up some leftovers from the fridge.

I eased myself off the sofa with a groan and hobbled over to the kitchen. With a bit of ingenuity I could piece together a half decent breakfast—rack of lamb with a redcurrant and balsamic vinegar sauce, some celeriac mash, braised squash and some petits pois and baby carrots.

I put my rushed breakfast in the oven to cook while I went upstairs for a shower. I noticed that Virgil had shredded a newspaper during the night, presumably out of spite for not having been fed while I was beaten, concussed and locked-up, etc. He was now sitting in front of the shredded newspaper, looking at me expectantly. The pieces of curling newspaper were set out in rows and looked strangely like a set of word puzzles:

he man is FBI What Not seems
accent my southern arse
jerry bonkers is neighbour
serial basement real look
material his in killer

If I hadn't been so tired, hungry and in need of a good bath, I might have passed the time seeing if I could make any sentences from the random words. As it was, I was feeling tired and understandably grumpy.

"Damn it, Virgil, you're so messy." I swept up the pieces of newspaper and emptied a can of tuna into his dish with bad grace. "It's been a really tough night and you're not helping, you know." I glared at him and stomped off upstairs for my shower.

Ten minutes under the scalding water and I was refreshed and ready to go. I bandaged my wounds, ate my rack of lamb breakfast, dried my hair and dressed—black bootleg trousers, black polo neck sweater, and black pointy boots with buckles. I felt like Catwoman. I looked more like Hippowoman. Downstairs, I picked up my handbag and flung in a few essentials—phone (damn, I'd need to remember to recharge it at some point), gun, cigarettes, Zippo, Tupperware container containing leftover rack of lamb—and set off for the office.

XXXXX

As I ran up the stairs, I could smell the aroma of over-brewed coffee, and hear Fifi belting out numbers from West Side Story in her throaty alto—courtesy of her 60-a-day habit, no doubt. Bless her, she'd already arranged for a carpenter and a glazier to fix the door to my office, and a painter was painstakingly painting back in 'HELENA HANDBASKET INVESTIGATIONS'. As he moved out of the way to allow me to enter the office, I stopped dead. Below, in smaller letters, read 'featuring Fifi Fofum—Psycho Sidekick'.

I grinned, shook my head, and straightened my face, trying to look stern.

Fifi was tidying my desk. I'd told her on several previous occasions that I didn't want the bottles of booze in my drawers in alphabetical order—I preferred them arranged by hangover-inducing properties.

Top drawer: gin, vodka, white wine, etc. Tequila, cherry brandy and cheap red wine—the heavy hitters— in the bottom drawer. She had a guilty look on her face and I wasn't sure if that was caused by being caught out in her booze-tidying task, or because she'd promoted herself from secretarial support to psycho sidekick. She was dressed with her new role in mind. She was still in femme fatale mode but instead of the usual slut-red suits and 40's dresses with the sweetheart necklines, she was wearing a severe black suit with a jacket boasting shoulder pads that looked like diving boards, and a long pencil skirt with a kick pleat. Her peep-toed black and white check shoes looked positively risqué in comparison with the severity of the suit. When she saw my various cuts and bruises her eyebrows, which were pretty scary at the best of times, rose almost to her hairline. Joan Crawford on crack cocaine.

"Good morning, Mommie Dearest," I said. "Been busy have we?"

"Basted?"

"What have I done to deserve that?" I was shocked.

"No, dollface. Last night, were you basted? You know—oiled, tanked, out on the roof? Did you tie a bag on? You look like you tried to carry a moose head through a revolving door."

"Oh!" Light dawned. "You mean was I drunk? No—I'll give you the short version. I'm getting a bit fed up of repeating the long one. I've been beaten up (twice), discovered a dead body, haven't had much sleep and then this morning at dawn the police carted me off down the hockshop." I was very proud of myself for using language Fifi would relate to, but she looked puzzled.

"Hockshop? Why would the flatfoots drag you to a hockshop? Did they think you'd hocked some hot ice or some oyster fruit?"

"Damn, I got that wrong, didn't I? They dragged me off to jail. Is that not the hockshop?"

"No, sweetcakes, you mean the hoosegow. The caboose, the icehouse, the jug, the sneezer. Did you get your elbows checked?"

"Errrr . . . actually, my elbows are probably the only part of me that don't hurt."

Fifi shook her head. "No, babe. Did the flatfoots slap the nippers on your lunch hooks and put you under glass?" She held out her hands, wrists together. She was either demonstrating being arrested, or suggesting some harmless sexual peccadillo. I plumped for the former.

"Yes, but they let me go. I had an alibi."

I caught a look of concern in her velvety brown eyes before she narrowed them, causing her false eyelashes to snap together like a Venus Fly Trap. She took my face gently in her right hand, turning it from side to side to survey the damage, and stroking my cheek with a talon painted in subdued burgundy. I didn't dare move in case she poked my eye out. "Was it the flatfoots that gave you The Broderick, after they had your biscuit snatchers in the bracelets?" She feinted a left hook, then a right. "They play a little chin music with you, the lousy goons?"

"No, Fifi, it wasn't the police who beat me up, although there was some brutality—but mostly relating to fashion. No, the first person to beat me up was some guy I met in a bar." She opened her mouth to speak and I could tell she was going to launch into chastising and incomprehensible references to my bad taste in men, so I broke in: "He wasn't a *date*, Fifi. He was a possible witness. I was just asking some innocent questions about Robin Banks and he set upon me as though I'd suggested he was a bank robber or something. The second person to beat me up was apparently this nasty serial killer. Oh, and in between, I almost got hit by a truck, so it hasn't been a very good night on the old health front really. The good news is that things are looking up on the romantic front."

Fifi led me to my chair and made me sit down while she stroked my brow. "Well sister, here's the lay. From now on, I'm your torpedo from hell to breakfast, so you're jake. Anyone messes with you while I'm onside has a head full of bees and that's flat."

Sometimes talking to Fifi made my head hurt. I wish she came with her own translator.

But I took it this was the part of the interview where Fifi told me why she was a suitable candidate for Psycho Sidekick—i.e. she was now looking after me and, while she was doing so, people would be stupid to think they could mess with me.

"But, Fifi, what about the danger aspect? How are you going to protect yourself, let alone me?"

Fifi looked hurt. "Dollface, don't vip another vop. I'm a black belt in Kung Po. Anyone threatens you, I'll be all over them like a cheap suit."

I didn't have the heart to tell her that Kung Po was a chicken dish involving cashew nuts. I sighed and gave in. "OK, you're hired."

Fifi squealed, clapped her hands and gave me a hug. "So boss, where's my roscoe?" She formed a gun with her fingers and blew on the tips. I shuddered. Fifi with a gun was not something I wanted to contemplate. Luckily, I was saved from answering by a knock at the door.

"It's open," I called. "Would you mind coming in carefully? I've just had it fixed."

Two elegant and well-dressed women opened the door and stepped into the office. The smell of expensive perfume replaced that of over-roasted coffee beans. Fifi introduced my visitors. "The cackle-broads I mentioned on the phone, boss."

"Oh yes—the cackle broads with the . . . errrr . . . jingle-brained tale of dipsy doodle?"

"The very ones, dollface. Cups of java all round?" I was glad to see that Fifi wasn't letting all her secretarial tasks fall by the wayside just because she'd suddenly become my hatchet man. I nodded at Fifi and gestured to the two women to sit down.

"Now then ladies, according to my associate, you have some confused tale of chicanery to tell me?"

The taller of the two women leaned forward intently. "Miss Handbasket, my name is Aurora deGreasepaint, and this is my sister Smilla daCrowde." If she hadn't told me they were sisters I would have guessed. Both had the same turned-up nose and big blue eyes—like a pair of matching Barbie dolls. That they both had Barbie's wasp waist, ultra long legs and gravity defying boobs, was something I tried not to feel jealous about, but it was hard. So? I never said I was perfect, did I?

"I understand Owen Banks came to see you yesterday?" Aurora deGreasepaint continued. "My sister and I thought it only fair to warn you that Owen Banks is not to be trusted. He's a lying scumbag. I was . . . am . . . was Owen Banks's girlfriend, and my sister here used to be the girlfriend of Robin Banks." Smilla daCrowde lowered her head and pulled a handkerchief out of her handbag, sniffing delicately as she did so.

This plastic doll with the pneumatic breasts was Owen's girlfriend? What did Aurora deGreasepaint have that I didn't? Well, apart from the obvious that is. I made a mental note to join a gym. As Smilla sighed and her bosom heaved, making her wiggle like a snake with nerve troubles, I also made a mental note to ask her for a recommendation for a good plastic surgeon, although now didn't seem like an appropriate time.

I removed a piece of paper and a pen from my stationery drawer. "So, you were Owen and Robin's girlfriends. This would be . . . what . . . five years or so ago? More?"

"Oh no, Miss Handbasket." Aurora deGreasepaint smiled slyly at me. "Is that what he told you? No, the last time Smilla and I saw Banks was a month ago. In a hotel at Heathrow airport."

"Which one?"

"The Travelodge. He always was a cheap bastard."

"No . . . which Banks brother?"

"Actually . . . both of them." She leaned back, an expression of spiteful glee on her face. "Together." Hers was an expression you could imagine Barbie having if Ken had just dumped her, and she'd gone round his house to have it out with him and he'd answered the door wearing one of her negligees.

I must have looked stunned, because she added, "I assume he didn't tell you that. What was his story? That he hadn't seen Robin for the last five years?" I nodded. "And, presumably, that he hadn't seen the diamonds at all? Well, I can tell you that he was just as involved with the jewellery heist as Robin. Maybe more so."

Her sneering voice was beginning to grate on me. OK, I wasn't a very good judge of men, and it looked as though I might have Owen Banks all wrong, but Aurora deGreasepaint was pouring salt into the wound with a cement mixer and grinding it in with a heavy duty salt-grinding machine.

"So, dear, he might have come over all innocent and coy with you—and I can see from your face that he did. But there's more to Owen Banks than meets the eye; he's way out of your league, honey, and I suggest you back off before you get hurt." The last part of the sentence—the bit after the nicely placed semi-colon—was hissed.

I tried to remain calm. "And may I ask exactly why you've come to see me?"

"Apart from to threaten you and add some much needed tension?" Aurora deGreasepaint stood up, and was swiftly followed by her silent sister. Aurora leaned over the desk and put her face close to mine. Smilla followed suit. One or both of them had eaten garlic the night before. Lots of it. "Stay away bitch." The words came out with all the speed and venom of an arrow dipped in curare. "Stay away from Owen Banks, and stay away from the jewels. They're both mine. And if you stick that big, interfering nose into my business any more, I'll chop it off and feed it to my fish." With that, Hannibal Lecter Barbie and her sister Harpo Marx Barbie turned and walked away.

"I do *not* have that big a nose. And don't slam the—"

Too late. The door slammed and a crack six inches long appeared in the freshly installed glass. If nothing else, this case was going to cost me a fortune in new doors.

Fifi came in from the anteroom with four steaming mugs of coffee. "Here's the java," she said brightly. She put them down on the desk and looked around the room, as though the sisters might be hiding in the middle of the dust storm that had been blown up by their departure. "Where are the twists?"

I opened one of the drawers and poured a healthy measure of Jameson's into one of the mugs of coffee with a shaking hand. "Some fucking psycho sidekick you are," I said.

CHAPTER TEN

(Messing Up A Crime Scene)

Leaving Fifi to call out the glazier yet again, I decided it was time to visit the scene of one of the crimes—Luke Warmwater's house—and also to visit the presumably grieving widow of Justin Case.

I got into my car and put The Flaming Stars in the CD player. 'Bring Me The Rest of Alfredo Garcia' started and I turned it up and drove off to 18 Laurel Court. As Frank Lee had promised, the key to Flat 1B was under the mat. I had promised not to disturb anything or touch any potential evidence but there was no way I could get inside without tearing off the crime scene tape in front of the door.

Inside the flat the curtains were closed and it was pitch black. Sweat broke out on my face. The heating was turned up really high, and there was the horrible coppery smell of blood that I was getting used to from my close proximity to it on more occasions in the last couple of days than I'd had hot dinners. But it still made me gag, as well as not want a hot dinner any time soon. I rummaged in my handbag for some Vicks—policemen on TV rub it under their noses when they have to deal with rotten smells. Unfortunately, I couldn't find any Vicks, but I had some toothpaste which I always carry just in case I get lucky, so I rubbed some of that over my top lip, and all around my nose, just to be on the safe side.

I turned on the light and stepped gingerly around the rusty coloured bloodstain on the rug in front of the door. The stain was shiny and still looked sticky. Lee had told me not to touch anything. I don't know why he nagged me at every turn. Did he think I was stupid? I turned down the heating, opened the curtains, and flung the windows open. There, that would let a bit of much-needed fresh air into the place. I waited a few seconds, but the smell was still making me feel queasy, so I rolled up the bloodstained rug, found a bin bag in the drawer and dumped the rug inside it. The rubbish bin in the kitchen hadn't been cleaned for some time, so I chucked that in the bin bag too, and dumped the whole lot outside the flat door for the bin men to collect later in the day. I opened a few cupboards and found a duster and some lemon spray polish and gave the place a good going over and, finally, vacuumed up. I did like things to be neat and tidy when I was on a hunt for clues.

The flat was small—a living room, kitchen, bathroom and bedroom. As the police had mentioned, posters of David Beckham covered almost every wall in the place. The bedroom didn't turn up anything other than a pile of dirty laundry, an unmade bed, and the largest stack of magazines I'd ever seen. I thought at first that this would be Warmwater's supply of porn, so I made myself a cup of tea, set out a plate of Hob-Nobs which I found in a cupboard, and curled up on an ancient bean-bag to have a quick glance through the magazines. Disappointingly, they all turned out to be about trains—with titles like 'Locomotive Monthly', 'Exciting Engines' and 'Big Trains'. I flicked through some of them—just in case there was a clue hidden between the pages—but I soon found that the only thing hidden between the pages was some kind of gooey substance —which I could only hope was mayonnaise—that was causing some of the pages to stick together. Before very long, I gave up in disgust.

The bathroom and kitchen were typical male bachelor pad type places—the barest of essentials in the cupboards, one pan in the kitchen, a fridge fully stocked with cans of beer, a drawer full of takeaway menus. I felt quite at home. I did notice one slightly odd thing—the toilet seat was down. I filed that one away for future reference.

The living room yielded slightly more in the way of useful information. A comfortable black leather sofa, a big screen TV and DVD player, and a fancy chrome sound system dominated the room. Unlike the rest of the flat, with its worn and dated furniture and decor, these things looked new. And expensive. A telephone sat on the low coffee table in front of the sofa. On the pad next to the phone a telephone number was scrawled. I turned the pad to face me and read the number. I knew that number! Now, if only I could dredge up from the depths of my mind where I had seen it before. Come on, Helena. Think. Nope. Nothing. I hated when this happened. It was so annoying.

On the pad I could make out the faintest imprint of a name, as though someone had written on the sheet of paper on top and then torn off the sheet. At last—a chance to do some real detective work like I'd seen on CSI. I needed to find a pencil. The cabinet holding the new TV and DVD player also had a number of drawers. Surely one of them would contain a pencil. Everybody owned at least one pencil. Most people had a whole drawerful. Not Luke Warmwater. After half an hour of frantic searching, all I'd found were some old shopping receipts, a tape measure with the first seven inches missing, a roll of very hairy Sellotape, some loose thumbtacks and half a dozen dodgy looking DVDs (*Hot Engine*, *Throbbing Metal*, *Tunnels of Desire* and *Long Hard And Steamy*—

and its sequels *Long Hard And Steamy 2* and *Long Hard And Steamier*). More train stuff, I assumed. I sat back down on the sofa, frustrated. I *really* needed to see what had been written on that top sheet of paper. How could Luke Warmwater *not* have a pencil?

It was then that I noticed the small case next to the notepad on the table. It said 'pencil case' in neat green letters. I tried it as a last resort and by pure coincidence, inside was a whole range of pencils. I picked out the sharpest one and gently rubbed the lead over the indentations on the paper, uncovering the words: Ring Helena Handbasket.

I gasped. Of *course* I had seen that number somewhere before. It was my own. Suddenly the reason that the name Luke Warmwater had meant something to me clicked into place as well. That was the name of the first strange man who had called me yesterday—the one who had said he had something to tell me and had then so rudely rung off part way through our conversation. Could the raspy voiced friend who had been so concerned about my health be the same Luke Warmwater who had been murdered here the day before? Or was it just a bizarre coincidence?

My heart beating like the hearts of a herd of pregnant sea lions being set upon by a starving polar bear with a headache, I looked around the room for something else which might give me a clue. As well as the phone, the coffee table was also home to a new-ish laptop. I opened it and switched it on. That was as far as my technical expertise stretched. I didn't know much about computers, but I knew a woman who did. I picked up the phone and rang my computer geek friend, Heidi Salami. When she answered, I heard the silvery tones of Doris Day optimistically chirruping away in the background about finding a pillow-talking boy.

"Heidi, I need you over here straight away. I've found a laptop and need to know if it contains any clues." I gave her the address.

"I'll be right over, Helena. In the meantime, don't touch anything. You never know what information you might destroy. I mean it, Hel. Don't touch one single key. Technology can be dangerous in the hands of idiots."

I was insulted that she could think I would fiddle with the computer.

She was as bad as Detective Lee. I promised her that I wouldn't touch the computer and replaced the receiver. Now, what was I going to do until Heidi arrived? I opened up the program from the Accessories— Games—Solitaire menu and started to play.

A quarter of an hour and two cans of beer later, there was a knock at the door. I let Heidi in. I was always struck by how much she looked like Shaggy from *Scooby Doo*, even down to the wispy beard. As I opened the door wider to let her in, she picked up her skateboard and tucked it under her arm.

"Don't want to leave this outside," she said. "It's the latest state-of-the-art, aerodynamic board."

I pointed her to the computer and she looked at me accusingly. "You've been meddling with it, haven't you?"

"No! Of course not."

"I would be more likely to believe you if 'Player' didn't say 'Helena H'."

I blushed. "So, what can you tell me?"

Heidi fiddled with some buttons and scowled at the screen. "Damn. It looks as though he deleted a whole heap of stuff yesterday."

"Can you get it back?"

She screwed up her face and made that sharp indrawn breath noise that electricians and plumbers make when they tell you that what you thought was going to be a ten-minute job involving a washer and a couple of screws, was actually going to involve you remortgaging the house and selling the kids into slavery. "Probably," she said, "but it might be tricky and take a while." She pressed a few mysterious buttons. "Here you go. Here are all the deleted files."

"Wow, Heidi, you're amazing. How did you do that?"

"I'm not sure if there's any point in telling you, since you won't understand all this technical stuff, but, basically, in layman's terms, I restored the Recycle Bin."

As she suspected, by the end of her sentence, I'd lost her. It was all too complicated for me.

"I'm going to have a look at his e-mail," she said. "There might be something in there that would help you."

"Great idea, Heidi. I wouldn't have thought of that." I watched her, mesmerised. "What are you doing now?" I asked.

"Opening up Outlook Express and going into his Inbox. There we are."

"I'm more familiar with Netscape. I don't like this. The layout's different."

Heidi sighed and pressed a button or two.

"That's better," I said.

He had eleven messages. I deleted the Nigerian spam e-mail, the Viagra offer, the 'make $60K in two days by sending this e-mail to seven million of your closest friends' e-mail and the e-mail from the Horny Housewife Sluts. Of the seven left only three looked remotely interesting. The most intriguing one was from a company called Perfect Match, offering to set him up with five dates for a small outlay of £750. I forwarded that one to my home e-mail address. One was from Robin.Banks@hotmail.com and was dated two weeks before. It read:

Hi Luke,
Just to let u know I'm going into deeper hiding. They're all after me. The diamonds are still hidden. No-one knows where they are, not even Owen.
Did you catch that game on Wednesday? That Beckham's a dickhead, mate. How could he have missed a sitter like that?
Oh, by the way, just thought I'd better tell you—one of the people after me is a particularly nasty serial killer. I think I may have misled the serial killer into thinking you know where the diamonds are. Hope that doesn't cause u any problems.
Robin

The final e-mail was dated two days before and was from SerialKillr 5093@yahoo.com

Dear Luke,
I'm coming to get you, you David Beckham worshipping heathen. I'm going to chop off your hands, carve a hole in your chest cavity and leave a small scarlet fish in the hole. Then I'm going to dump you in the woods so that small woodland animals can nibble at your toes. But you won't care by then because you'll already be dead.
Love,
SerialKillr5093

Heidi was breathing down my neck. "Anything interesting?"

"Not sure. This might be spam too. But I'll take the laptop with me and have a better look later." I switched the laptop off, unplugged it, and tucked it under my arm.

"Won't the police want to take the machine into evidence?"

I looked at her and grinned. "Whatever for, Heidi? Really, leave the investigating to me, and you just concentrate on the geeky stuff. The police won't want to see this. I'm not even going to mention it to them."

We left the flat and I locked up after us, sliding the key back under the mat again. As we got to my car, Detective Lee pulled up behind me. I walked over to his car and he scowled at me.

"What's all that white crap on your face?" he asked me.

"Toothpaste," I told him. "Duh."

"What the . . . Never mind, I'd rather not know. Anyway, I hope you didn't disturb anything in there, or remove anything, Handbasket."

"Of course not," I said indignantly, looping the trailing wire of the laptop around my wrist and adjusting the computer under my arm. "And I put the key back under the mat just where I found it."

He nodded brusquely and got out of the car. "I'm just gonna have a look around, check for clues, dust for prints, splash some luminol around."

"Oh, well, actually, I've already done that."

He stopped in the act of locking his car door and looked at me, raising his eyebrows. "You dusted for prints?"

"Well," I said, "more like . . . just dusted, really."

"Jeez, Handbasket. I wish you'd leave this to the professionals. I might have to arrest you again, just to keep you from interfering. Where are you going now?"

"I'm going to drop Heidi off and then I thought I'd interview Justin Case's widow, Charity. Have you spoken to her yet?"

"Nah. We'll get around to her one of these days. We're just a bit busy down at the station. Apart from this serial killer thing I've got my superior on my ass about all the outstanding paperwork—crime figures, expenses, all that shit. And all of it in triplicate." He rubbed his stomach. "No damn wonder my ulcers are getting worse, my wife left me and my kids hate me." He ran his hand over his face, then said, "Anyway, Handbasket, just keep your damn nose out." He strode off towards Luke Warmwater's flat.

"Detective Lee?" I called after him.

He carried on walking.

"Do you think my nose is big?" I couldn't hear his response clearly. It almost sounded as though he'd said 'Fuck you and your big nose, you big-nosed, nosey bitch' but I was sure that I must have misheard.

As we drove to Heidi's I asked her for some suggestions for some technical stuff that might come in handy around the office. "I don't have much money and I'm a bit of a technophobe, but is there some cheap, simple equipment that you could set me up with?"

Heidi thought for a moment. "Sure. I'll nip down to Dixon's tomorrow and get you some bits and pieces. Satellite phone, wireless fax modem, Global Positioning System, tracking device, pager, binoculars, digital camera disguised as a lighter, walkie-talkie watch, two-way radio, pocket PC, night vision scope, digital camcorder, electronic listening device, infrared thermometer gun, flashlight stun gun, electronic lock pick, hot dog griller and bun warmer. OK?"

"Just get me a couple of everything. Will they take a lot of time to learn to use?"

"Not at all. I can show you how to use the whole lot in . . . ooooooh . . . five, ten minutes."

"Great, bring it all to the office tomorrow and I'll give you some cash."

I dropped Heidi off at her Mum's and drove to Justin and Charity Case's house, which turned out to be a smart detached house on a leafy cul-de-sac. I rang the bell and the door was opened by a starched-looking woman who was wearing a black skirt dotted with white flowers, and a white ruffled blouse, buttoned up to the neck.

"Mrs Case? I'm investigating your husband's death . . ."

She opened the door wider. "Oh, I've been wondering when the police would be here. You were here faster when we were burgled a couple of months ago. Come in. Please wipe your feet. I just had the carpet cleaned."

The best thing to do was to let her think I was with the police. It wasn't lying exactly, just not telling the absolute truth.

I followed her into an immaculate sitting room filled with dark-wood furniture that looked as though it had been in the family for generations. The print of the woman with the blue face that had so worried me as a child when it hung on my grandmother's wall dangled over the fireplace here. I realised that the painting still worried me now. What strange disease did the blue-faced sitter have, and why did the artist waste possibly valuable time painting her, when he could have been rushing her to hospital? Charity Case motioned me to sit down on what was probably the most uncomfortable sofa I've ever sat on. It was small and hard and covered in a busy chintz print. The padding was stingy—as though whoever had stuffed it didn't want anyone to sit on it for too long. Everything about the room was designed for discomfort. There was one plant, an African Violet—which, on closer inspection, proved to be made of plastic—numerous small dark tables, each with a perfectly positioned crocheted doily, and one shelf of Reader's Digest condensed books which looked as though they'd never been opened. I felt as though I'd stepped back into the 1980s. All that was missing was The Human League standing in the corner singing 'Don't You Want Me Baby'.

Both Charity Case and the hard chair she was perched on had upright, straight backs. Her hands were clasped tightly around her knees and her face had a pinched look to it.

"Mrs Case, I'm sorry to intrude on you at this sad time, but I just need to ask you a few questions."

She nodded, her mouth pursed as though words were expensive and she wasn't going to let any out before making sure she wasn't wasting them.

I took out my notepad. "Can you tell me when you last saw your husband?"

"Yesterday morning. Just before he went off to work."

"Where did he work?"

"He was an accountant. For Stubezzi Enterprises."

I looked up from my notepad. "Evan Stubezzi?" She nodded. Goodness me—what a strange coincidence. What were the chances of *that*, I wondered.

"Did he seem at all worried or upset about anything leading up to his murder? Any strange phone calls, unexplained absences—apart from nights spent with his mistress of course?" Perhaps that had been a tad insensitive. Luckily, she didn't appear to notice.

She thought for a moment. "No, nothing. He left the house as normal yesterday, kissing me on the cheek and telling me he'd be home in time for dinner. Of course, he was a little later than normal leaving the house, due to the phone call from a man with an electronic sounding voice—you know, as though he had one of those voice-disguising gadgets. Either that or Stephen Hawking had got the wrong number. I was listening on the upstairs extension and this gentleman told my husband that if he didn't tell him where the diamonds were he'd kill him and leave his handless body in a woodland clearing. But, no, nothing out of the ordinary."

It was frustrating. I just couldn't get a break in this case. "I'm sorry to ask this but . . . well, the note in your husband's mouth referred to . . ." I trailed off. The steely look in her eye reminded me of my old headmaster, a man who inspired fear in all but the most belligerent pupil.

"Yes", she said shortly, her mouth opening and closing like a steel trap. "Adultery." She pronounced the word in four distinct, bitter syllables, as though she was spitting out something foul-tasting. "And with his secretary, of all people." Her face screwed up in distaste, as though she had just taken a bite out of a wasp. "I would have expected him to have had a better sense of propriety."

What? An affair with the boss's wife would have been acceptable on the social scale, but a lowly secretary wasn't?

"Could you give me his secretary's name, Mrs Case?"

She looked at me suspiciously. "You should already have her name. I left a message for a Detective Frank Lee, who I understand is in charge of this case. I want that Whore of Babylon arrested for my husband's murder. Do you not speak to each other at that police station?"

"Well, I'm not exactly . . ."

The rest of the conversation was rather distressing for at least one of us, and I'd much rather draw a veil over how I was thrown out of the house after being lashed by her tongue—and not in a good way. Despite that, the visit had been worth it, even though I knew I would have nightmares about the blue-faced woman, Mrs Case and, above all, the Reader's Digest condensed books. As well as the obvious lead about Justin Case's affair, I also felt as though I had learned something else of importance, which I was going to keep to myself for a little while longer. If only I had known how vitally important it was, I could have solved the case right there and then, and averted another death.

CHAPTER ELEVEN

(Random Acts Of Senseless Violence)

I decided to go round and see Owen Banks. We could have a good laugh over everything that Aurora deGreasepaint had told me about him—all those nasty things that she had expected me to believe. Although I had only known him for just over twenty-four hours, I felt that we were soul mates and that we were destined to be together forever. I thought how serendipitous it was that his girlfriend, Barbara Seville, had been blown up in that unfortunate car explosion the night before, thus leaving the path clear for our happiness. One of those *schadenfreude* episodes that are the cause of so much *freude* at someone else's *schaden*.

When I arrived at Owen's it was 1 pm. Perhaps we could drive out to the country for a romantic lunch somewhere. A new BMW was parked in the driveway. I ambled up the path and knocked on the door. It took ages for Owen to appear and when he did he looked dishevelled. He was tying the belt of a faded bathrobe, his greasy, lank hair covering the top part of his face. His breath smelled of fish. Perhaps he'd had a tuna sandwich for lunch. I thought again how handsome he was.

"Hi, Owen. New car?"

"Helena! What are you doing here? Ummmm, yes, it was just delivered last night."

"I thought I'd come round and update you on the case. Aren't you going to invite me in?"

He blocked the doorway. "Well, errr . . . actually I'm a bit busy at the moment. Can you come back in a few days?"

"Owen, darling," a voice trilled from upstairs. "Come back to bed, honey. I've only got a few hours before I need to be back at the BMW dealership. I have another car to deliver."

"Owen, if the next words out of your mouth aren't 'Helena, would you like to come in and meet my mother, who works for the BMW car dealership?' I shall be thoroughly pissed off." I peered around Owen's hulking figure blocking the doorway and saw a slim, gorgeous woman who didn't look like anyone's mother, let alone Owen's, gliding down the stairs in one of Owen's shirts. You might think I'm exaggerating but, I swear, she glided. And how could she look so gorgeous after spending the night in the sack with a man? My man. If I were to wear one of Owen's shirts I would look like a half-naked bag lady. This woman looked like a model.

"Ummm, Helena, I'd like you to meet my new girlfriend, Augusta Wind. Gussie, this is Helena. She's the PI I hired to look into Robin's death. I was telling you about her—you know, the slightly odd woman? She has some news for me," he said apologetically.

Augusta Wind looked me up and down and, apparently, found me not much of a threat. I automatically smoothed my hair and thrust out my chest, but I knew I couldn't compete. "Well, sexpot," she said, "why don't I nip down to the shops for some more champagne, while you have a chat with your little friend, the PI." She grabbed him by the front of the robe and drew him close. "And when I come back we can pick up where we left off. Keep the bed warm for me." She winked at him, picked up the keys and wiggled her fingers at us in a way that made me nauseous. She gave Owen a long sloppy kiss and patted me on the head. "'Bye, Harriet." She loped off like a gazelle towards Owen's new car.

"It's Helena," I snapped at her as Owen dragged me inside. "Isn't she going to put a pair of your trousers on too? It's freezing out there."

Owen shut the door. I followed him sullenly towards the living room and plonked myself down on the sofa. He seemed distracted, and I was inwardly seething. He lifted his head as the car door slammed and the throaty growl of the BMW started up, followed swiftly by an enormous explosion which shook Owen's house and flung me on top of him, which I couldn't help feeling was rather nice, even though something told me that Owen had just lost another car and another girlfriend.

"Sorry, Owen. That must really suck. Twice in twenty-four hours as well. Who'd have credited it?"

Owen shrugged philosophically. "Thanks, Helena. I'm so glad I hadn't had either of them long enough to become attached to them." I was impressed with his optimism. So many men would have let this double double-tragedy get them down. Owen just bounced back. I did like a man for whom the glass was always half full.

XXXXX

Leaving Owen to call his insurance company, the BMW dealership and the police, I decided to pay a visit to the police station myself. If I was lucky, I would get to share some ideas with Detective Lee and Agent Art Ifarti (their ideas, not mine of course). If I was unlucky, I would get myself arrested again. Either way, I would get a decent cup of coffee and a couple of donuts.

I arrived at the police station and waved to the man who always sits at the counter. If that was what police work was like, even I could do that job. He buzzed me through. "Just go on up, Miss. I'm sure they'll be happy to see you. The serial killer incident room is at the top of the stairs, through the double doors, and at the end of the corridor."

As I walked along the deserted corridor I heard raised voices in an office to the right. The nameplate on the door read 'Chief Inspector Angus Beef'.

"Look, Chief. I've told you before. I'm a maverick, loner cop. I don't work well in a partnership. Sometimes I think you're just here to make my life hell. And if you keep breathing down my neck the whole time and giving me pointless assignments I'll never get anything done. Now, how many donuts do you want me to get?"

Angus Beef mumbled a response and Frank Lee stormed out of the office with a face like thunder. His eyebrows lowered still further when he saw me and he growled, "What the fuck do you want, Handbasket? You're the biggest pain in the ass it has ever been my misfortune to encounter." My heart jumped at the sight of him, and his endearing way of talking to me just made me like him even more. Although I had only known him for just over twenty-four hours I felt that we were soul mates and that we were destined to be together.

"Hello, Detective Lee. I was on my way to see you. I thought we could get together and pool our information."

He grunted and strode off down the corridor. I practically had to run to keep up. He opened a door on which a piece of paper had been pinned. It read 'Seriel Killer Incident Room'. I opened my mouth to mention the rather obvious spelling mistake, but a glance at Lee's face told me that this might not be a good time.

In the incident room a sizeable crowd of police was gathered, standing around chatting and drinking coffee. Three large white boards at the end of the room were covered in writing in black, blue and red felt-tip pen and there were numerous photos of the two dead men, the woodland dumping sites, and the crime scenes themselves, plus a photo of Robin Banks and one of his hands stuck to the boards. When I say 'one of his hands', I mean a photo of one of his hands—not one of his actual hands. There was also a map with lots of little multi-coloured pins stuck into it, and someone had drawn a maze of black lines leading between the photos, the map, and the writing. It all looked very impressive. As I approached the board, I noticed that the map was of Sierra Leone, but I'm sure there was a good reason behind that.

"It's nice to see so many police keen to get involved in this case," I said to Lee.

"What are you on about now?" He folded his arms and gave me his trademark affectionate glare.

I gestured at the room full of police. "All of these men, ready and alert and wanting to get on with the investigation."

"Actually, this is the break room. We didn't have any spare offices in which to set up the serial killer incident room." He clapped his hands. "OK, guys. Clear out and give us some space."

Everyone in the room filed out, grumbling. "All this for some lousy serial killer," I heard one of them say as he threw the remains of a donut in the waste-paper basket. I wondered if the donut was salvageable.

Soon there was just Detective Lee and me left in the room. "This is it?" I asked, stunned. "You're the whole team?"

"Unfortunately not. You're forgetting Golden Balls."

"Hey, Ms Handbasket. How you doin'?" The southern drawl of Agent Art Ifarti brought out the strange Pavlovian response it had provoked before. Although I had only known him for just under twenty-four hours I felt that we were soul mates and that we were destined to be together.

I blushed. "I'm fine, thanks, Agent Ifarti. And please, call me darling . . . errrr . . . I mean Helena."

"Likewise, Helena. Call me Art. And maybe when this horror is all over, we can go out and get us a passel of chicken fried steak, some okra and a heap of grits."

"That sounds wonderful." I had no idea what he'd just invited me to, but I hoped it was something we could roll around naked in.

Detective Lee snorted. "If you two have finished flirting, I'd like to solve this case. Here's what I've discovered so far." He opened a file and sat on the edge of a desk. "First of all, it looks as though Luke Warmwater may have been an old friend of Robin and Owen Banks from way back. We're still trying to find further evidence of that, but initial indications suggest that they knew each other before the jewel heist. I was hoping that we'd maybe find a computer and access his e-mail, but it looks as though he was PC-less, although there *was* an empty laptop case in his living room, which was a little strange. I've put in a request for his phone records over the last couple of months, but, of course, it will be a while before we can get those." He paused, scanning his file, and I made a mental note to get Heidi to pull Warmwater's phone records for me. I knew that was something she could do in just a few minutes, although she'd keep banging on about it being illegal.

Lee continued. "Warmwater had, until recently, been working at Stubezzi Import Export, a division of Stubezzi Enterprises. A coincidence, but nothing more, I'm sure of it. He was sacked about a month ago. We're not sure why yet, but it's unlikely to be material."

The detective turned a page and tapped the file. "Now, on to Justin Case. He had been having an affair, as the piece of paper with the 'Thou Shalt Not Commit Adultery' Commandment seemed to indicate. He had been seeing Emma Roids for the last year or so. She was his secretary at Stubezzi Enterprises. We'll need to get round to interviewing her at some point in the next few weeks. Again, it's something we can put on the back burner for a while—we've got plenty more important clues to be chasing down."

"Like?" I asked.

He scratched his ear with a long, slim finger. "Like where the killer is buying those small red fish, for a start. We have every fishmonger in town staked out, I've got men on all the fishing clubs hereabouts, and we've brought the local fish and chip shop owner in for questioning. And two of my officers are interrogating the vicar, trying to get to the bottom of these biblical references." He looked at Agent Ifarti through narrowed eyes. "Some of us do *real* police work. We don't just make shit up and ponce around in sunglasses."

He paused to check his notes and I jumped in. "Detective, what is Emma Roids' address?"

"I'll write it down for you, but I don't want you going round there and pestering her. She's very upset, and this has nothing to do with you. I'm not sure how many times I need to tell you to keep your nose out."

"And a purty cute nose it is too, Helena," said Art.

At last—someone who didn't have something nasty to say about my nose. Honestly, a girl could get a complex about all this.

"Finally," said Lee, "the body of Robin Banks was found just over an hour ago in a woodland clearing. His hands were chopped off. Which, of course, we already knew. A hole had been cut into his chest and a small scarlet fish sewn into the cavity, and in his mouth was a piece of paper with 'Thou Shalt Not Steal' written on it. I assume that the Commandment is a reference to the stolen diamonds. I think we can safely say that our serial killer has now claimed a total of three victims."

Damn. Owen would be devastated. "Any idea where Robin Banks' body has been all this time?" I asked.

"No. He'd obviously been kept somewhere because the pathologist, Katya Fallingstar, said that he's been dead a few days. The odd thing is that he's really, really cold and very stiff. It's as though he'd been put in a freezer. Very strange."

"Hmmm, maybe you could find out who's recently rented a cold storage unit, Detective Lee. Or if there are any local cold storage businesses with dodgy proprietors," I suggested.

Lee slapped his forehead with his palm. "Damn it, Handbasket, that's a great idea. Why didn't we think of that? I'll get onto it straight away." He closed his file. "Anyway, that's all I have. Not much, but we're making headway. We need to catch this man before he kills again, and we still have two pairs of hands we need to find. What's most puzzling is that this killer is choosing his victims seemingly at random. There's no pattern, no method to his madness. I really can't link these murders. All we've got are three men with absolutely nothing in common: Robin Banks, who, five years ago, allegedly stole thirty million in diamonds from Evan Stubezzi; Luke Warmwater, friend of Robin and Owen Banks who was sacked by Evan Stubezzi a month ago; and Justin Case, Evan Stubezzi's accountant. Nope, I just can't see a pattern. Anyway, we'll have to put that aside for a while. Agent Ifarti, what do you have for us?"

Art Ifarti cleared his throat and went up to the white board. "Well now, Detective, loathe as I am to point out to y'all that y'all is wrong . . . well, y'all's wrong. There *is* something which links these three men." He paused dramatically and looked at us over the top of his sunglasses. "All three of them were found in woodland clearings, all three of them had their hands chopped off and removed, all three of them had a hole cut into their chests and a small scarlet fish sewn into the cavity, all three of them had one of the Ten Commandments written on a piece of paper and tucked into their mouths." He paused and looked at us expectantly.

"And . . .?" Lee encouraged him to continue.

"What do y'all mean, 'And . . .?' That's it. Y'all said there was nothin' linking these three men. I've just proved to y'all that there is. What more do y'all want?"

Lee stood up and moved closer to Ifarti, jabbing his finger in his face. "Look, pal. I'm sick and fed up of you Feebies coming over here and treating us hardworking cops like the poor relations, and coming out with all your psychological bullshit. This case is going to be solved with good old-fashioned pavement pounding and police work, not by some psychic mumbo jumbo that doesn't mean squat."

They squared up to each other like a pair of strutting peacocks. Lee was shorter but more heavily built. Ifarti was older but lean and fit-looking. The reek of testosterone filled the air like that of a sweaty jockstrap which has been left in a gym locker overnight. You may wonder how I know that, but there's a reason I was banned from the local gym, OK? There was some shoulder pushing, the usual 'Wanna step outside?', 'Yeah, you and whose army?' posturing and posing until eventually I stepped between them.

"OK, guys, break it up. There's no need to fight over me like this. I appreciate that this is a love triangle here, but let's behave like adults, OK?"

They looked at me and then at each other. Frank Lee shook his head "Fighting over . . . Jeez, Handbasket, sometimes I really think you're away with the pixies. Alright Ifarti, what else have you got?"

"Well, in addition to the valuable information about this killer that I gave y'all yesterday, I've been studying his MO. This whole Ten Commandments thing points to a religious mania and a father complex. I think when y'all find y'all's killer there will be a basement in his Aunt Sally's house, which he keeps locked. In it y'all will find the walls plastered with photographs and newspaper clippings from all the cases, as well as lots of biblical references. He will have numerous copies of the Bible around the house and he will quote it at any opportunity. He will also keep a small refrigerator in the basement and in there y'all will find all y'all's missing hands. The hands are symbolic of his father's hands. His father used to beat him when he was a child, but y'all's killer is torn between love and hate for the father who beat him and who left him when he was ten years old. He was brought up by his mother, along with his six sisters. After being left by her husband, the killer's mother, a very religious woman who washed her son's mouth out with soap while quoting the Bible, struggled to make ends meet and this poor boy had to wear his sisters' cast-off clothes." Art shrugged. "So he grew up to be a serial killer who's killing his father over and over again. It's no wonder really."

"And where do the small scarlet fish come into it?" said Lee.

"Well, I'm still working on that one, Detective. I'll tell y'all as soon as I work it out. It will be something deep and meaningful, no doubt. It may be the clue that cracks the whole case."

Lee snorted. "Well, we'll see, shall we, Ifarti? Do you want to have a little wager as to which of our methods catches the killer first?"

I coughed gently. Had they forgotten me in all this? Who was to say that *I* wasn't going to be the one to catch the killer?

Frank Lee turned to me. "So, what about you, Handbasket? We've told you all this highly secret information that we're not supposed to share with the general public. You got anything for us in return?"

I thought for a moment, recalling the two psycho sisters, Aurora deGreasepaint and Smilla daCrowde, and their threats and insinuations—including the fact that Owen Banks had possibly been lying when he said he hadn't seen his brother for five years. Then there was the computer and the strange e-mails at Luke Warmwater's, plus the fact that it was possible that Warmwater had phoned me just before he died to tell me that he knew something important about Robin Banks. There was also my visit to Charity Case and the coincidental but possibly vital information that her husband had received a telephone call from Stephen Hawking the day he died. Plus the whole really weird exploding car/girlfriend combo of Owen Banks. And finally the niggling feeling that was tickling the back of my mind that there was something a little odd about my neighbour, Jerry Mander. I shook my head. "Nope, not a thing, Detective."

A policeman knocked on the open door and Lee motioned him to come in.

"Guv, some woman just called. A Miss Emma Roids. Says she was the mistress of Justin Case and she has something really, really important to tell you about his death and how it all links in with that big jewel heist you investigated five years ago. She wants someone to go round and interview her straight away. She says if you don't go round and see her and get this important information, then the serial killer will strike again tonight."

Lee sighed. "Well, I can't do it. I need to go out on a donut run for the Chief and then I've got to do these sodding expenses forms that Head Office have been on to me to do for the last four months. Ifarti? You wanna go round and interview her?"

"No, I need to study my textbooks and see if I can find out the psychological significance of these fish. I don't think there'll be anything to be gained from interviewing this woman, but y'all knock y'allselves out."

"Handbasket? What about you?"

I yawned. "Well, I'd love to but I'm a bit tired. I'm going to head off home. I haven't slept for thirty-six hours, and I need to take another aspirin for the dislocated knee, the broken ribs and fractured jaw and stuff. Besides, I'm starving." I looked at my watch. Where had the day gone? I couldn't believe it was already 7 pm. The supermarket would have closed and I still hadn't had a chance to do any shopping. Looked like I'd be eating leftovers again tonight.

Had we but known what was going to happen that night, we would all have gone round to Emma Roids' house straight away. Our communal decision to put off interviewing her would turn out to be a huge mistake. But how were we to have known that from her telephone message? If only she'd been clearer and more specific.

CHAPTER TWELVE

(Turning Up The Heat Under The Protagonist)

I drove in an exhausted daze. It had been another fun-packed day. I couldn't wait to get home, take a shower, have something to eat and then collapse into bed. As I got out of the car, my neighbour Jerry Mander stood up from where he had been sitting on a deckchair in his front garden reading the Bible.

"Hi, Helena. That's a nice sweater you're wearing. I used to have one just like it. Well, it originally belonged to one of my six sisters of course, but eventually it got handed down to me after our father left us when I was ten, and our mother couldn't afford to buy us new clothes any more. Would you like to come and see my basement? I've done it up real nice."

"Oh, Jerry, I'd love to, but some other time maybe? I'm so tired that I'm just going to go in and take the phone off the hook and get to bed."

He looked disappointed. "I'd really like you to see it."

"Well, how about Sunday?"

"Sunday?" Jerry looked shocked. "But Sunday is a day of rest. You know what the Bible says?" He held up the battered book, like a fire and brimstone preacher in the pulpit. "It says in here: 'And on the seventh day, God took a nap.' If more people read the Bible and heeded its words, this world would be a better place. I'm disappointed in you, Helena." He stomped off into the house, slamming the door behind him.

My gaze remained fixed on the door for a moment and then I shrugged and let myself into my own house, switching on the lights, dumping my handbag and shoes, and undoing the zip on my trousers as I entered. I went into the kitchen to make myself a Blood Transfusion to try and pep myself up. I filled a highball glass three quarters full of ice cubes, poured in an ounce of vodka and an ounce of dry sherry, added five and a half ounces of tomato juice, the juice of one lime and a couple of dashes of Worcestershire sauce. I sprinkled a pinch of celery salt over the whole thing and floated a one-ounce layer of Fernet-Branca on top.

As I turned to go and collapse on the sofa in the living room, I noticed that Virgil had knocked over a half-used tin of Alphabetti Spaghetti and the contents had spilled all over the floor.

The little pasta letters had fallen out of the tin willy-nilly so that they formed little groups of letters:

"Oh, Virgil. That was my dinner, old son. What the hell am I going to eat now?" I mopped up the messy mixture of pasta shapes and tomato sauce and fed Virgil a tin of Goat Liver and Sheep's Eyeball cat food. I was so hungry, I was almost tempted myself. I opened the fridge. Hardly anything in there and none of it looked appetising. I pulled out a few of the scant items and knocked myself together a makeshift snack: garlic and ginger crusted salmon served with potatoes dauphinoise, mango and tomato salsa and a noisette of spring greens. It was a mismatched selection, but it would have to do. While it was cooking I dug an old sachet of 'Glint of a Tint' out of the bathroom cabinet and dyed my mousy brown hair what was laughingly described as 'succulent chestnut' on the carton. It came out more of a 'stale carrot'.

By the time I'd dried my hair, eaten dinner, typed up my case notes on the computer, downloaded my e-mail and checked out the Perfect Match website mentioned in the e-mail I'd forwarded to myself from Luke Warmwater's computer, it was just after midnight and I was shattered. Checking over my notes, I had little to show for the day (unless you counted the five potential dates from Perfect Match). I had a shower, made myself a pitcher of Whisky Sour (a bottle of bourbon, a freshly squeezed lemon and one egg white) and retired to bed.

I was woken about half an hour later by a thumping in my head. The Whisky Sour jug was empty, but I never usually had a headache after normal consumption such as last night's. Maybe it was because I'd mixed it. I'd known the egg white was a mistake when I put it in the jug. Then I realised that the thumping was actually coming from the front door.

I looked at the alarm clock. 1 am. Somehow I didn't think that this was a social call. I pulled my .38 out from under the pillow. Then, just to be on the safe side, I pulled out the *.22* as well. I left the Uzi, the sawn-off shotgun and the rocket propelled grenade launcher there just in case.

I put on my tattered dressing gown and crept downstairs and towards the front door, my heart beating ten to the dozen. As I reached the door there was another knock.

"Who is it?" I called. My shoulders were tense as I remembered the telephone message from Emma Roids, warning of another murder. Maybe the serial killer had changed his MO and was coming after women now. My knees started to shake and my teeth to chatter.

"It's me, Jerry."

I let out my breath, relieved. Not the serial killer after all. Just my slightly odd neighbour. I slid the .38 into my dressing gown pocket and opened the door a crack.

"Jerry, what are you doing here this late? I was in bed."

He shouldered his way through the door, and smacked me round the face with his Bible. I fell, cracking my head on the table and awkwardly twisting one leg. I was sure I could feel one of the bones snapping. I managed to get out my .38 from where I had stupidly put it in my dressing gown pocket, and got off a couple of shots. But Jerry, too, had a gun and soon bullets were zinging around the room like mosquitoes on acid. I took a hit to the shoulder and, when I dropped my gun, Jerry grabbed me and held me down, kneeling on my chest. I wrestled an arm free and hit out at him and then I brought up my head and cracked him under the chin. He staggered off, bleeding. I grabbed his legs and yanked and he smacked down to the floor like a mackerel on a fishmonger's counter. But as bad luck would have it, he fell on top of me, pinning me to the ground once more, and crushing my windpipe. I decided it was time to give in gracefully.

"OK, Jerry. Get off, please. I'm feeling light-headed and weak."

He panted, his breath hot on my face, his hands caressing my neck with murderous fervour. "Well, you know what the Bible says about the weak."

"What does it say?" I croaked, flailing ineffectively at the hands around my neck.

"The weak shall inherit the earth."

"Meek," I said.

"What?" He relaxed his hold on my throat for a few seconds.

"It's the meek that shall inherit the earth."

Jerry tightened his hands. "Don't be ridiculous. Who's going to give the earth to the *meek*?"

Before I blacked out, I wondered what it was that the meek had done so wrong and the weak had done so right.

XXXXX

I woke up who knows how long later. How come the only sleep I was getting recently was after I had been concussed or strangled? I was blindfolded, gagged with some nasty tasting item that might have been a dirty sock, and my hands and ankles were tied together behind my back. I knew for sure that I wasn't in my own house. The floor was hard and cold and the place felt damp and smelled mouldy and stale. Every part of me ached and body parts I didn't know I had were squealing in pain. My head was throbbing and I felt sick. I tried to spit out the gag—I was afraid I would throw up and choke on my own vomit.

By turning myself over onto my stomach and rubbing my face into the floor, which felt like rough concrete, I managed to loosen the gag enough so that I could spit it out. I lay for a few seconds taking huge gulping breaths of musty air before considering how to extricate myself from the ropes binding my hands and feet. If I hadn't been in so much pain, I would have been impressed at my flexibility. The knots were tight and the rope strong and I despaired of ever managing to free myself. I sobbed hopelessly, frustrated and annoyed. How could I never have realised that my next-door neighbour was a serial killer? Had the clues to his depravity been there all along? If so, how could I have missed them?

I was going to die a horrible death. Without hands. Suddenly I remembered the Paul Daniels Magic Kit that my dad had bought for me when I was seven. Surely there had been something there that might help. I dredged long-forgotten memories of family magic shows through my fuzzy brain. Let's see. There was the Making A Coin Disappear Into Thin Air trick, the Vanishing Knot On The Handkerchief trick, the Pouring A Glass Of Water Into A Newspaper trick (I never managed to get that one right somehow and Mum eventually banned me from doing it in the living room). Ah! And there it was, the Escaping From Being Hog-Tied With Ropes trick. I'm not at liberty to divulge how the trick works, or I will be thrown out of the Paul Daniels Mini Magic Circle but, after squirming about a bit and twisting various body parts, I finally managed to free my hands. From there it was easy enough to untie my ankles. Of course, it would have been easier still if I'd left my ankles tied until after I'd taken my blindfold off, but my excuse was that I was still groggy.

Free at last, I sat considering my new wounds. A broken nose, twenty-five broken ribs, eight broken fingers, enough bruises on my body that if you joined them up they would spell 'compound fracture of the tibia'. In Latin. And I'd been shot in the shoulder. Nothing serious, then. I did a few sit-ups and some one-armed bench presses and squat thrusts to ease out my knotted muscles and looked around the room. I guessed that I was in a basement.

A bare bulb in the ceiling threw a weakly flickering light into the room. I shivered in the dank air. I no longer had my dressing gown on, but I was still wearing my Winnie The Pooh pyjamas. I didn't think I'd been ravished. At least, I hoped not—it had been a long time since my last ravishing and it would have been just my luck to have been unconscious while it was happening. There were no windows and the walls were covered in photographs, newspaper clippings and scribbled notes, which I couldn't quite read. In one corner was a wooden staircase I presumed led to freedom. In the opposite corner sat a fridge. Wonderful. My mouth watered at the thought of a can of lemonade and I hauled myself to my feet and staggered over to the fridge. I opened it, reached my hand in and pulled out a hand. Since the hand was wearing a wedding ring, I knew it wasn't mine. I screamed and clapped a hand in front of my mouth to silence myself. Unfortunately, it was the one with the wedding ring, so I dropped it with another scream. If I hadn't realised it before, I knew now that I was in deep shit.

I looked at the walls. The newspaper clippings were from the three serial killings, and the photographs were of the three dead men: Robin Banks, Luke Warmwater and Justin Case. I didn't need to be told who the two pairs of hands in the fridge belonged to. The handwritten notes on the walls had Bible quotes on them: 'It is more blessed to take than to give', 'Give us this day our dairy spread', 'In the beginning was the Word, and the Word was Supercalifragilisticexpialidocious'. For a religious nutter, I suspected he didn't know his Bible quotes very well.

I heard the ominous sound of a key turning in the door at the top of the basement stairs. Isn't it funny how a normal, everyday noise can fill you with dread all of a sudden? I hurriedly wound the rope around my ankles and wrists and lay back down on the floor. I didn't have time to put the blindfold and gag back on, but I hoped, mad as a hatter as he was, that Jerry Mander wouldn't notice. He clumped down the stairs and squatted down beside me.

"I'm sorry about this, Helena," he said. "I just wanted you to see my lovely basement and you were always too busy. So I had to resort to drastic measures to get you here. I hope I didn't hurt you too much." He waved an expansive hand around his domain. "What do you think?"

"It's very nice, Jerry. Now would you let me go home?"

"Oh, I can't do that, Helena. I'm going to keep you here for a little while. You're too busy to spend time with me so I thought, well, if Mohammed won't come to the fountain, then the fountain will have to come to Mohammed."

"Mountain. It's mountain, not fountain." As soon as I'd said it, I could have bitten my tongue.

"Helena, you have this terrible habit of correcting people. It's very rude, you know."

I gulped. "Sorry Jerry. I won't do it again, I promise." I cast around for something to change the subject. "So . . . errr . . . why did you kill those men?"

He looked at me, puzzled. "What men? How could you think I could kill anyone?"

I gestured with my head towards the walls. "What about the photos and the press cuttings?"

"I like to keep up with the local news. If you'd come to visit my basement last year when I wanted you to, you would have seen the clippings of the local fête. But I papered over them with all this serial killer stuff. It's so much more exciting."

"But what about the hands in the fridge?"

"I found them."

"You found them?" He expected me to believe that? What was he—nuts?

"Yes, I saw someone leaving them on my doorstep yesterday. So I brought them down here and put them in the fridge."

By now, I was losing my patience. "Oh, and what did you think they were, Jerry? A gift from God? Who put them on your doorstep?"

My mad next-door neighbour stood up. "Helena, I think you're a little bit grumpy because you haven't had a lot of sleep recently. I'll give you the benefit of the doubt and let you get a few hours kip." He shoved the foul sock back in my mouth. "I'm going out for a few hours. The person who left the hands on my doorstep left me a nice little note asking to see me in the woods. I'll be back in the morning and I hope you're in a better mood then, and we can have a nice chat."

"Mmmmmmmmmmm, mmmmmmmmmmm."

"Goodbye, Helena." He ran up the stairs and out of the basement door, locking it behind him. I heard his muffled voice. "Aunt Sally, if you hear any strange noises, don't go down there. It's a big horrible rat. I'm just going to nip out and get some rat poison. For Lo, the Lord madeth the beasts of the field—all except the rats, which were a horrible mistake."

As soon as I heard the front door slam shut, I shook off the ropes and pulled the sock out of my mouth. I stumbled up the stairs and banged on the door at the top. Sally Mander was still in the kitchen. I heard her gasp and drop something on the floor. As it smashed on the tiles she squealed.

"Sally! It's me—Helena Handbasket. Can you let me out? Did Jerry leave the key in the door?"

There was a few seconds silence and then I heard her shuffling over, her slippers slapping against the tiled floor of the kitchen.

"Sally? The key. Is it there?"

"Go away, rat. Leave me alone."

"Sally, it's Helena, not a rat. Let me out. Please!" I rattled the door.

She shrieked and backed away. I heard her banging into the kitchen table.

"Rat! I'm going to bed and I'm taking my hearing aid out so that I can't hear you."

Shit. I collapsed onto the top step, sobbing. I had to get out. There must be something in the cellar which could help me. As much as I disliked doing it, I went back down the stairs. I looked carefully around for anything I might have missed. And then I spotted it.

On the wall next to a handwritten quote saying, 'Let he who is without sin, bake the first scone' was a rack with some carefully labelled tools and implements: 'hacksaw', 'chisel', 'pliers', 'wire', 'paintbrush', 'spare key for the basement door'. Yes! I grabbed the chisel, the pliers and the wire. Using the pliers, I cut a length of wire and fashioned a make-shift lock pick which I stuck into the keyhole and jiggled it up and down a bit, while poking the chisel into the space between the door and the jamb. Fifteen minutes later I was sweating and still jiggling the damn wire and shoving the chisel into the damn space between the damn door and the damn jamb. This was so much harder than it appeared on TV. On TV people broke into places all the time with nothing more than a hairgrip. A hairgrip! Of course. I dropped the chisel, pliers and wire, and took a hairgrip from my pyjama pocket. Thirty seconds later I was out of the basement door, across the kitchen and out of the front door, faster than a ferret down a greasy pole.

I dashed into my house to call the police, but first I had to make myself a cocktail to calm my nerves. At a time like this, only a large Zombie would do. I took down a highball glass, decided it was too small and emptied the flowers and water from the large vase on the kitchen counter. I poured in two ounces each of white rum, golden rum and dark rum, one ounce of cherry brandy, one ounce of apricot brandy and six ounces of pineapple juice. I added four ounces of orange juice, three ounces of papaya juice, an ounce of lime juice and a dash of almond syrup. I stirred the whole concoction, crushed some ice and filled the vase almost to the top. Then I floated an ounce of 151 proof Demerara rum on top and garnished the drink with a slice of orange, a slice of lime and a sprig of mint. I collapsed on the sofa and drank.

Half an hour later I called Detective Lee at the station. They told me he was out on a case but that he would call me back. Ten minutes later my phone rang.

"What the hell is it, Handbasket? I'm up to my elbows in blood and guts here, you know."

I burst into tears. "Frank! I've just been strangled, shot, kidnapped, imprisoned and made to eat a sweaty sock. But I know who the serial killer is. It's my neighbour, Jerry Mander."

There was silence on the other end of the phone. "I don't think so, Helena."

"No, really! He confessed everything . . . sort of. And he has the hands in a fridge in his basement, and stuff on the walls, just like Art Ifarti said. Of course it's him."

"Sorry, Helena, but your neighbour isn't the serial killer. We've just found Jerry Mander in a clearing in the woods with his hands cut off, a hole carved into his chest and a scarlet fish sewn into the cavity."

"That doesn't prove anything! It could be a ruse to throw you off the scent."

"No, Helena. He's dead."

"Oh, my God. That means there's a copycat somewhere out there!"

"Nope, it's the real deal. He even had a piece of paper tucked in his mouth with one of the Ten Commandments written on it." I could hear the crackling of a piece of paper. "Here it is: 'Thou Shalt Not Keep Body Parts In A Fridge In The Basement.'"

I thought for a moment. "Was that actually one of the Ten Commandments? I don't remember that one. There was one about not killing, but I'm not sure that the Bible ever mentioned fridges."

"Jeez, Helena. Who do you think I am? The Pope? Who the hell has read the Bible all the way through? In a book that long there must be *some* mention of white goods."

I noticed that since I'd told him about being kidnapped, he'd been calling me Helena rather than Handbasket. He must have been worried about me. I wondered what a cop's salary was like, and whether I could afford to give up work once we were married.

"Helena?"

I shook my head to get rid of the fantasies—the white picket fence, the 2.3 children, the family holidays, the regular sex. "Damn . . . and I was sure I'd solved the case through good detecting skills, cunning, and the sheer good luck of being kidnapped by the suspect. Where are you now?"

"Just arrived at the crime scene. We're waiting for the police photographer and the forensics boys and for Dr Fallingstar to pronounce Jerry Mander dead before we can start looking for evidence."

I was puzzled. "I thought you said he *was* dead. Is there a chance that he might still be alive, then?"

"None whatsoever. Why?"

"Well, you said you were waiting for Katya to pronounce him dead. If there's any question about it, oughtn't you to call an ambulance rather than a pathologist who'll cut him open and pull out his still beating heart before you realise it's too late?"

Lee sighed. "It's procedure, Handbasket. You should leave this investigating business to the professionals, you know. You're obviously not cut out for this sort of thing. Until the pathologist has pronounced the victim formally dead, and forensics have been all over the scene, we don't touch anything, and I mean anything. We treat the crime scene very carefully. We don't let anyone get close to the body, or disturb any evidence. We need to preserve it so that the forensics boys can do their thing using all that technological shit—you know, the machine that whirls things around in little glass bottles, the printers that produce lots of pretty coloured graphs, and those clever little insects that can tell you how long a person's been dead. Hell, we've even got someone back at the lab firing guns and checking the striations on the bullets."

"Oh, I didn't realise that any of the victims were shot as well as hacked about and stabbed."

"They weren't. We're cops. We just like playing around with guns. Some sort of penis extension thing apparently."

As we had been chatting on the phone, I'd been dressing. I'd put on a casual pale blue mini skirt and matching lace blouse, and a pair of denim platform sandals. A bit retro, but perfect for a night in the woods. "I'm on my way over right now, Frank. Don't let them take the body away until I've seen it."

CHAPTER THIRTEEN

(Tampering With The Evidence)

It was 3 am by the time I arrived at the woodland clearing—my second in twenty-four hours. The body was draped over a log and a scarlet fish was peeping out of the chest cavity—well, it would have been peeping if it had still been alive. The familiar lined paper with the Commandment on it lay next to the body.

Frank Lee, Agent Art Ifarti and two other policemen were standing around chatting. Lee introduced the two cops to me. "The little guy here is Hugh Mungus." Hugh raised his hand in salute. "This old guy is Lou Gubrious. Lou's just a couple of weeks off collecting his pension. Been with the Force thirty-nine years."

Lou smiled and nodded at me. "Can't wait. I'm buying a boat with my pension money and me and the wife are going to sail all over, docking where the fancy takes us. Haven't had a holiday for twenty years, so I'm certainly going to enjoy my retirement." He looked as though he could do with a long holiday. He appeared to be about eighty years old. Obviously the awful things he'd seen, the stresses and strains of policework, the years of staring death in the face, had all taken their toll.

"Thirty-nine years," I said. "I'll bet you've seen some changes."

Lou Gubrious stared off into the distance, wistfully. "Yeah, I remember the good old days. Wish we could have them back."

"You mean the friendly bobby on the beat, being able to leave your front door unlocked when you went on holiday—that sort of thing?"

He stared at me, frowning. "No. I meant the days when we could beat the crap out of suspects and they didn't go around bleating about their rights and the Police And Criminal Evidence Act. Fuckin' wimps."

Detective Lee laughed. "The changing times never stopped you over the years, Lou. Anyway, Handbasket. Don't touch a thing, OK?"

"Alright," I snapped. "You've made yourself perfectly clear. I won't move. I won't even breathe. God, do you think I'm thick or something?" I stomped over to the log where Jerry Mander's body was lying, shoved the body along a bit and sat down.

"Shit," said Lee, rummaging through his pockets, a cigarette dangling from his mouth. "I haven't got a light. Sergeant Mungus, have a look through the victim's pockets and see if he has matches or a lighter, would you?"

"Sure, guv." Hugh Mungus hesitated. "Should I walk carefully round these footprints that lead to and from the body, just in case they're the killer's? The footprints leading to the body are a lot deeper than the footprints leading away. It's as though the person was carrying something heavy, which he put down right where the body is, before walking off again."

Frank Lee waved the hand holding the cigarette at him. "Nah, don't bother. They'll be nothing. Just get me a light, would ya?"

Mungus felt in Jerry Mander's pockets. "Sorry, guv, no matches." I remembered I had my 'Vixen' Zippo and threw it over to Frank Lee. Mungus continued to rummage in the pockets. "But there's something here." He took out a piece of paper and smoothed it. "A note. And it seems to be written on the same paper that was in the vic's mouth." He picked up the paper lying next to the body. "Look, guv, the two pieces fit together exactly. Do you think it's a clue?"

Lee shrugged. "Could be." He held out his hand for the paper from Jerry's pocket and read out the message written on it "'Meet me in the woods at 2 am. Don't tell anyone you're coming, especially that big-nosed neighbour of yours.' Wow, have a look at this, guys." He handed it to Lou Gubrious, who studied it before handing it to Art Ifarti, who passed it to me with a smile.

I held it, my face blushing. I could feel them all staring at my nose.

Lee looked at the other policemen. "Anyone got any of those little bags we put stuff in that we want to keep?"

"Evidence bags?" Mungus patted his pockets. "No, sorry. I was in such a hurry to get to drive the police car that I rushed out without picking any up." Lou Gubrious shook his head, and Agent Ifarti just looked as though all this was below his radar.

Frank turned to me. "Handbasket, would you mind taking the note home and looking after it until I come back on shift tomorrow afternoon?"

"Sure," I said, putting it in my handbag. As I leaned down to put my bag back on the ground, I spotted something glinting in the bushes off to my right. I got up, tripping over Jerry's feet and falling onto his body, knocking it completely off the log. "Whoops." I walked over to the bush and parted the branches. Hidden inside was a distinctive samurai sword with a serrated edge. The entire length of the sword was coated with blood, so I picked it up by the handle and brought it out of the bush. "Look at this." The blood was dripping from the blade. I took a tissue from my pocket and wiped off the blood. It would be a real bugger to get out of my lace blouse.

"Wow." Hugh Mungus whistled. "Let's have a go." I handed him the samurai sword and he wielded it in front of him, adopting the stance of an Olympic fencer. "They had these in that film we watched round yours that time, Frank. Remember?" He thrust the sword out in front of him, making chopping motions.

"*Seven Brides for Seven Samurai*? Great film," said Lee. "I really like all those Japanese films—*Kagemusha, Crouching Tiger Hidden Dragon, Godzilla*. And Kurosawa is amazing."

I couldn't believe it. Another thing we had in common. "Me, too!" I said. "I love Kurosawa—well, all Japanese food, really."

Before Lee could answer, Katya Fallingstar appeared in the clearing, flanked on either side by two men clad in the unattractive all-in-one white suits of the forensics experts—like a nightmare vision of The Osmonds singing 'Crazy Horses'.

"Helena, dahlink." As Katya kissed me on both cheeks, I smelled the off-putting scent of formaldehyde and stale stomach contents. She'd had it bottled, and dabbed it behind her ears whenever she left the morgue. "You haf another corpse for me? How kind." She bent and reverently studied the body of Jerry Mander.

"Dr Fallingstar," said Lee, hovering over her shoulder, "can you give us an approximate time of death?"

"Now, Detective, you know better than that. I will not be able to say for certain until I get him into the lab and slice him open with my lovely sharp knives."

Lee shrugged. "I know, but I have to ask. It's traditional. Is there anything you can tell us right now?"

"Well, he is definitely dead, if that helps." She flexed Jerry's right leg. "Rigor has either not set in, or has worn off, and, by the lividity, he was not killed here, but has been moved. It would appear that he has been stabbed. And there is another of these fish. It, also, is dead. Would you like me to autopsy the fish too, yes?" Katya looked up at the sky, where the first indications of dawn were beginning to show. "Now, if you don't mind dahlinks, I need to get this body back to the lab quickly. Daylight is not good for my skin."

The white-suited men took photos, checked around the body for clues and, finally, zipped the body into a black nylon bag and we all left the clearing. Katya placed a possessive hand on the body bag and gently remonstrated with her assistants as they unceremoniously manhandled the body. "Take care of this poor boy. He has suffered indignities enough, yes?"

Back at the cars, Lee turned to me. "I guess I'm not going to be able to stop you sticking your nose in, am I, Handbasket?"

The nose stuff was beginning to get on my nerves now. Lee would have to stop it once we were married, otherwise he'd be on his fifth divorce within a year. No wonder his other wives had all left him, if he was so persistently insulting about their slightest flaw. "If you mean am I going to continue with the investigation, then yes, I am. It's personal now. Jerry was my neighbour and a really good one too. Alright, so you could argue that he was a little off balance, but he was harmless. Well . . . maybe not exactly harmless, but he'd never do anything to anyone without good, if bonkers, reason."

Lee nodded. "Right. Well, I may still decide to arrest you again. Quite frankly, your alibi for the time of Jerry Mander's murder is a little weak, to say the least." He held up his hand to stop my protestations. "Yes, I know. You say you were locked up in his basement, but do you have any witnesses? Any proof?"

I thought for a moment. "Actually, I do. I spoke to Sally Mander and asked her to let me out. And you'll find my fingerprints all over stuff in the basement, including the hands in the fridge."

He nodded. "I'll get round there now and question Mander's aunt. Have a look at this basement you keep banging on about before I head off home for a sleep. But I warn you, if things don't stack up, then I'll be reading you your rights and throwing you back in the slammer. Your cell's all ready. We still haven't erased your name from the board outside the door."

"Oh . . . whatever." Blah blah blah. Anyone would think I was a hindrance, rather than a help. I looked at my watch. It was just coming up to 7.30. I could get an early start in the office, try out the new equipment Heidi was bringing round, and then see what Justin Case's mistress, Emma Roids, had to say. "I'm going to nip home and hide this note somewhere clever."

"Great." Lee handed me the samurai sword. "This is a bit bulky. Can you take it home along with the note? They're both important pieces of evidence. Keep them safe and bring them down to the nick some time in the next couple of weeks."

"Will do." I took the sword and got into my car. "See you later."

X,X,X,X,X,

I pulled up outside my front door and got out of the car. I opened the front door and Virgil looked up at me from the hallway, one back leg cocked behind his ear as he cleaned his bottom. It was a skill that was both appealing and appalling. I shook my head and stepped over him.

Now, where could I hide the note and the sword? I needed a place where no one would ever look. Virgil watched me through his one slitted eye. "Where, where, where, Virgil, old son? If only you could talk, I'm sure you'd come up with a great idea." I made myself a cup of fresh tea while I was waiting for inspiration to strike. As I was drinking it, I heard a clatter from the kitchen and ran in to see what the noise was. Virgil was sitting with a guilty expression on his little face. The canister of loose tea had fallen off the counter. Virgil must have swished his tail in the tealeaves because it almost looked as though words had formed from the leaves.

the evidence mattress under put don't your
roids emma dodgy is
bank see can account you look a get if her at

What a mess. "Virgil, I just don't know what's got into you these days. You're so clumsy." I got out the dustpan and brush and swept up the tealeaves. Then I finished my tea, picked up the note and samurai sword and wandered around the house looking for a suitable hiding place. Of course! I had the perfect place. The very last place anyone would think of looking. Under the mattress. How come I hadn't thought of that straight away? I must still be suffering the ill effects of my night on my mad neighbour's basement floor. The samurai sword was still a little dirty, so I dunked it in a sink full of bleach and scrubbed off the rest of the bloodstains. I didn't want to get my mattress dirty. I pushed the note and the sword under the mattress until they were out of sight. Now I could relax and forget about them.

XXXXX

Fifi hadn't yet arrived when I got to the office, so I unlocked the freshly glazed door, noticing that the small 'featuring Fifi Fofum—Psycho Sidekick' had been replaced by 'STARRING FIFI FOFUM—PSYCHO SIDEKICK' in bright red letters larger than those that said 'HELENA HANDBASKET INVESTIGATIONS'. I made a mental note that the next time the glass in my door got broken, I would deal with it myself, before I was relegated to the sidelines in my own business.

I had just sat down at my desk when Heidi Salami staggered in, her arms filled with boxes. She was out of breath and sweating. "I'll just nip back down to the skateboard and bring up the rest," she said.

I thought of something I'd been meaning to ask her. "Heidi, before you do, is there any way you can hack into the FBI's website?"

She scratched her nose. "Sure. What is it you want to see?"

"Their personnel files," I said. I could feel my cheeks heating up. "I'd like to look up the records of a Special Agent Art Ifarti. We have this . . . connection . . . and I just want to make sure he's the right man for me. He says he's not married, so I just want to check that, and also, I have no idea what sort of salary an FBI agent gets, so I wondered if you could hack into his employment details."

"Helena, a child could hack into the FBI's files." She came around to my side of the desk, switched on my computer and dialled up the World Wide Web, or whatever it was called. In Google she typed 'FBI + "personnel files"' and a screen came up which said, 'Hi, welcome to the FBI Personnel Department's Home Page. Please type your username and password.'

"Shit. I guess that's that then," I said.

Heidi snickered, covering her mouth with the frayed cuff of her sweatshirt. She spotted a mustard stain on her sleeve and scraped at it before doing some more secret hacking stuff. "It'll just be a couple of minutes." She licked her lips. "There you go." She pushed the keyboard over to me and went back downstairs to bring the rest of the electronic equipment up.

I typed in Art Ifarti's name and waited for his details to appear. The screen flashed: 'No Match Found'.

"So, why do you need all this stuff anyway?" Heidi had reappeared, stacked the boxes on the floor in the corner of the room, and thrown herself into the chair on the other side of the desk. She crossed her legs over the chair's arm, and unwrapped a half-eaten hamburger which she proceeded to tuck into, taking tiny mouse-like bites, her cheeks doing a rumba as she chewed.

"Hmmmmm? Oh, the gadgets?" I shrugged. "I just thought they might come in useful." Maybe I had spelled his name wrong. I clicked on the tab which said 'click here to see the names of all our agents in alphabetical order'. Iddell, Ifan, Iffley, Ignatius. Not an Ifarti in sight. "This is really weird, Heidi. He doesn't appear to be listed."

She stopped chewing and raised her eyebrows. Someone should tell her they were badly in need of plucking. "That *is* odd. Let me have a look." I moved out of the way so that she could sit down and hack into some more secret US government websites. She chewed on her nails and muttered to herself, "Weird. He's got to be here somewhere."

Finally she sighed and sat back in the chair, silent for a moment, her face screwed up in puzzlement. She shook her head slowly. "Sorry, Helena. I've checked the Social Security, every state and city telephone directory and reverse directory, fingerprint records, hospital records, alumni and school records, birth records, military records, drivers licence records, FBI, CIA, AFIS, DMV, IRS, EPA, NCIC, NYPD, CSI, VICAP and RSVP. There's no such person as Art Ifarti."

I was stunned. First the hints from Aurora deGreasepaint that Owen Banks was not all he seemed, and now this. Why were the men in my life such a bunch of lying toe-rags? Oh well, at least I still had Detective Lee and my first Perfect Match date who I was meeting for lunch later (Hal Litosis—who, according to his resume was an extremely handsome, fit, blue-eyed 32-year- old, 6'3" millionaire businessman with all his own hair and teeth, too romantic for his own good, sensitive, caring, liked children; hobbies included going to the gym, skiing, eating out, commitment, long walks on the beach, nights in front of roaring fires.) At least Frank and Hal weren't lying to me.

I wondered whether I should tell Detective Lee about Special Agent Art Ifarti (or whoever he was). Perhaps I'd tell him when I took the samurai sword and note down to the police station. As long as I remembered to, that is.

Heidi and I unpacked all the equipment she had brought for me. She told me what they all were as we took them out of the boxes and admired their shiny surfaces and clean lines: satellite phone, wireless fax modem, Global Positioning System and tracking device, binoculars, pager, digital camera disguised as a lighter, walkie-talkie watch, two-way radio, pocket PC, night vision scope, digital camcorder, electronic listening device, infrared thermometer gun, flashlight stun gun, electronic lock pick, hot dog griller and bun warmer. She spent the next ten minutes showing me how to use it all, apart from the GPS system which we put aside to install in my car when we went downstairs. To be honest, I didn't concentrate as much as I should have done, as my mind was elsewhere. Apart from the sheer duplicitousness of Art Ifarti I also realised that I hadn't given any thought to what I was going to wear for my lunch date with Hal Litosis. But all the technology looked relatively straightforward, and I was sure I would pick it up as I went along. The only one I'd worked out pretty quickly how to use was the hot dog griller and bun warmer.

I held up one of the more complicated pieces of kit. "Thanks a lot, Heidi. That was really helpful. Could you just show me how to switch this one on again? How do I use it?"

She looked at me with that sort of long-suffering look I get from people a lot for some reason. "You don't need to switch them on, you just look through them. Like this." She put them up to my eyes. "They're binoculars."

"Whoa—everything looks so big! That's amazing. Wow, I'm going to love all my new toys. Anyway, how much do I owe you?"

"£17,985.76. Call it a round eighteen grand?"

"Sure. I'll get Fifi to pay you out of petty cash when she comes in." We went downstairs and installed the GPS thingamajig.

"So, what exactly is a Global Positioning System and what does it do?" I asked her as she lay under the steering wheel column, fixing the small black box.

"Well, in simple terms, it's a navigational and positioning system developed by the U.S. Department of Defense, by which the location of a position on or above the Earth can be determined by a special receiver at that point interpreting signals received simultaneously from several of a constellation of special satellites. It's a navigation system made up of between eighteen and twenty-four satellites, each carrying atomic clocks, and which provide a receiver anywhere on earth with extremely accurate measurements of its own three-dimensional position, velocity, and time and is used to determine latitude, longitude, and elevation anywhere on, or above, the Earth's surface. The system involves the transmission of radio signals from a number of specialized satellites to a handheld receiving unit. The receiving unit uses triangulation to calculate altitude and spatial position on the Earth's surface. Error in the accuracy of GPS derived positions can be introduced through the nature of local conditions. These errors can be greatly reduced using a technique known as differential GPS. So, it's a satellite technology that uses mathematics to calculate the position in three dimensions (latitude, longitude, and altitude as I said) of something on the Earth by measuring the time it takes for the satellite's radio transmissions, travelling at the speed of light, to reach a receiver on the ground. It requires a fleet of satellites in space. Applications of the GPS technology—as well as determining a position on the Earth, of course —include measuring the Earth's movement after an earthquake, or locating drop points for airlifted relief supplies. GPS location accuracy is within twenty meters. Location accuracy can be boosted through the use of Wide Area Augmentation System (WAAS) or Differential GPS (DGPS)."

I was silent for a moment, as I took it all in. "That's great. I've always wanted something that . . . errrr . . . did all that."

Heidi tightened the last screw and pulled herself upright. "You don't have a clue what I just said, do you?"

"Well, to be completely honest . . . no."

She scratched her nose with the screwdriver. "OK, how about this then? A GPS will get you from point A to point B without getting lost."

"Ah! Got it. Like a taxi driver?"

"Yeah, just like a taxi driver only it will take you straight there, won't drone on about the football, and you don't have to give it a tip."

"Great. Can we try it out?"

"Sure, Hel, just tell it where you want to go."

We climbed into the car and shut the doors. I switched on the ignition and the GPS. "Hello GPS, this is Helena. If you don't mind, I'd like to go home and get changed for my lunch date." Nothing happened. I looked at Heidi. "Why are you sobbing like that?"

"You can't just *speak* to it. You have to program in where you are now, and the address that you want to go to." She reached over and showed me. "There, now. Shit, better go, I've got a date in half an hour."

"Heidi! You've got a *date?*"

She pulled her hair over her face in her embarrassment. "It's an online Role Playing Game. I'm Princess Doris and he's my knight—Sir

Rock of Hudson. I haven't ever seen him, but we've been dating online for about six months now. Today we're going to take it to the next level." She went bright red and raised her hands in front of her mouth, as though she was trying to force the words back inside.

"Heidi! You mean . . .?"

"Yes. We're going to cross over The Bridge of Unheavenly Steps and slay The Dragon of Looberon."

I was obviously missing something here. "And then once you've slain the dragon you'll have sex in his lair?"

"Helena! That's terrible." She giggled, patting my hand. "No, the love that I and Sir Rock of Hudson have for each other is pure and innocent. Oh, Hel, I love him so—he's handsome, and fearless and brave and chivalrous." She hugged her knees and her eyes shone. Suddenly my geeky friend Heidi didn't look like Shaggy from *Scooby Doo* any more. She looked ethereal and Princess-like, sitting in her tatty sweatshirt and cut-off jeans. I was so pleased for her. I gave her a big hug. Before I let her go I took her shoulders and put my face up close to hers.

"Heidi, if Sir Rock of Hudson turns out to be Lord Shit of Dungheap, let me know and I'll shove his family crest so far up his arse . . ."

She hugged me again. "Thanks, Hel, but don't worry about me and Sir Rock. He's wonderful and wouldn't hurt me for the world." She got out of the car and onto her skateboard and disappeared off down the road. I hoped she was right. As I watched her happily skating off I prayed that Sir Rock of Hudson wouldn't turn out to be a spotty thirteen-year-old from Scunthorpe.

I drove home, my new gadget telling me which way to go. Of course, I knew the drive home very well, but it was nice to have it confirmed with the latest technology. Once indoors it took me an hour to choose an outfit that was suitable for my casual lunch date with Hal Litosis. After due consideration I selected a see-through white mesh blouse, a black leather mini skirt with a side split, and thigh-length black boots with four-inch heels. I didn't want to be too obvious, but I also hoped there was enough flesh on show that he wouldn't look too closely at my nose. The only thing I was worried about was that the outfit was a bit over the top to go and interview Emma Roids. Having said that, I wasn't quite sure what the fashion etiquette actually *was* re interviewing the secretary-slash-mistress of a murdered man, but then I didn't think Emma Roids would either, so I decided that the slut blouse slash mini skirt slash thigh high boot combo was just as good as anything else in my wardrobe.

Back in the car, I programmed in my address and the address for Ms Roids which Detective Lee had given me earlier. She lived on the other side of town and I followed the instructions of the GPS. The instructions took me past the new shoe store I'd seen the other day. I was fully intending to drive straight past, only slowing down briefly for a quick look, but I saw the most delicious pair of brown suede mules, which I thought would perfectly replace those that had been destroyed earlier following my pond dunking. I turned into a side road and immediately the clipped metallic voice on the GPS tracking system said, "Please turn back onto the High Street."

"Just a second." I jumped out of the car and ran round to the shoe shop, scooped up a pair of the brown suede mules in my size, added a pair in black, a pair in lilac and a pair in fluorescent orange for good measure. I paid for them and dashed back to the car where the voice was saying, "I said get *back* in the car and turn *back* onto the High Street."

Unfortunately, the street I was on was a one-way street, so I had to drive to the end and loop in a circle to get back onto the High Street.

The GPS berated me all the way. "What the hell are you doing? Turn left. I said *left*. Get back on the High Street. You should be on the High Street. Are you listening? Can you hear me, you geographically challenged fool? The High—" I switched the damn machine off and rummaged in the glove compartment for my A-Z. At least it wouldn't talk back.

XXXXX

I pulled up at the address that Frank had given me but I wasn't sure I had the right house. If I had, then Emma Roids appeared to be doing very well for herself. Her boss, Justin Case, had had a pretty nice house, but Emma's was far superior. She lived in a mock Tudor mansion in the best part of town set in a couple of acres of land. It had a sweeping driveway with two cars parked in it—a year-old Porsche and a new shiny Range Rover.

I got out of the car and opened the wrought iron gates at the end of the driveway. Two stone statues of Pekinese dogs, probably three times as large as life, stared down at me from the gateposts, their little stone tongues hanging out. I climbed back in the car and drove up the gravel driveway and, as I parked, two smaller flesh-and-blood versions of the stone dogs ran around the side of the house, yapping and growling. These, however, were in fancy dress. One was wearing a neat red bow on its head, the other a green one. Both had fancy collars studded with rhinestones and each dog had an identical supercilious sneer on its face.

"Ruby, Emerald—come to Mummy," called a babyish voice from the back garden.

I opened the door of the car and stepped out, as a petite, attractive woman rounded the corner. She was wearing a short pale green robe and matching furry high-heeled slippers. Her black hair was piled on top of her head in a loose bun.

"Please excuse my babies," she said, scooping up the dogs, which were quivering with excitement. "They love to talk to visitors, don't you my darlings? Yes you do, yes you do, Mummy's precious little girls." I wasn't sure which was more nauseating, the baby talk, or the fact that the dogs were nuzzling and licking her mouth as she spoke. Obviously, the way to this woman's heart was through her dogs.

"They're gorgeous," I said, hoping I sounded sincere. I gestured to the stone dogs on the gate. "Are they . . .?"

"Yes, I had my cuddly bunnies immortalised in stone. Don't they look sweet?"

I nodded, hoping I looked sincere. "I'm sorry to bother you, Miss Roids. My name is Helena Handbasket. Can I ask you a few questions about Justin Case?"

"Ooooh, are you from the papers? Did you bring a photographer? Perhaps you could take a photo of me by the swimming pool looking sad and cuddling my puppies?"

"Actually, I'm a private investigator. I was hired by a client to look into the death of his brother who was killed in the same way as Justin Case."

Her face closed up and she hugged the dogs tighter. "I've never heard of Robin or Owen Banks, and I didn't have anything to do with the diamond heist. I wasn't the one who set it all up for them, telling them when the diamonds would be arriving and making sure that Evan Stubezzi would be otherwise engaged. Now, please leave."

Had I mentioned Owen and Robin Banks or the diamond theft? I didn't think so. There was something odd going on here. Emma Roids obviously knew more than she was telling which, quite frankly, wasn't very much. I would have to dig deeper—try to get her to open up.

"Miss Roids, did you know someone called Luke Warmwater?"

"I don't know what you're talking about. I never knew anyone called Luke Warmwater who recently got sacked from Stubezzi Enterprises. And he didn't have anything to do with the diamond heist either. He wasn't the getaway driver and he wasn't at all involved in finding a safe place for Robin Banks to run to."

It was no good. The woman was as close-mouthed as a clam with its jaw wired shut.

"Was Mr Case—?"

"Oh my God! Will you stop browbeating me! I wasn't blackmailing Justin and it's horrible of you to even suggest that I was. How dare you say that I made him embezzle funds from the company and use it to keep me quiet by buying me this house, these cars, a wardrobe of smart clothes and three holidays a year in the Canaries."

"Do you—?"

"Look, if you think I'm blackmailing all the top executives of Stubezzi Enterprises and that I have a number of accounts in false names at various banks in town then you're wrong. *So* wrong."

"Would—?"

"Oh, you're such a horrible bully. Here." She thrust a piece of paper at me. "Those are the names of all the people I'm blackmailing, and the reasons I'm doing so, along with all the bank account numbers and false names and PO box numbers I use." She burst into tears.

I sighed. It was obvious she wasn't going to tell me anything. I was wasting my time here.

She rushed past me, sobbing. She said, "I'm going to meet someone. I'm not going to tell you where I'm going and don't follow me."

I followed her to the Porsche. It was clear that my ancient old car was never going to keep up with a Porsche. As she started the engine I banged on the window. "Where are you going?"

"I'm not going to tell you. Don't follow me to Stubezzi Industries Head Office at The Stubezzi Building, number 15 Valley Forge Business Park or I'll call the police."

She was a tough nut to crack. Sometimes, being a private investigator was hard work. Other times, it was just really boring. Now and again, I got to do some really cool stuff like cut eye-shaped holes in newspapers and sit in hotel lobbies.

She screeched off down the driveway, churning up a cloud of dust and gravel. I would have been impressed by the Porsche's power had she not had to stop before reaching a speed of ten miles an hour to open the gates. I jumped into my own car and roared off behind her. At the bottom of the drive she turned left towards Valley Forge Business Park and shot like a shiny yellow bat with number plates out of hell. I don't like to use well-worn clichés like that, but that's exactly how it happened.

Damn. I had lost her. I asked the Global Positioning System where she was headed, but it didn't answer. I was on my own.

CHAPTER FOURTEEN

(A Pointless Personal Interlude
In The Life Of The Protagonist,
or How To Up That Word Count)

I drove slowly into town. It wasn't worth going into the office before I met Hal Litosis, my lunch date from Perfect Match, so I decided to call at my local coffee shop. A couple of cream buns would help coat my empty stomach so that I could eat like a bird at lunchtime—I didn't want to put Hal off by eating too much. The bird I was striving to emulate was the hummingbird, rather than the vulture, of course. So maybe three cakes would be better. I picked out a cream horn, a coffee meringue, and a chocolate and caramel éclair and ignored the shop assistant's flippant "Only three today, Miss Handbasket? Is there anything wrong?" remark. I ate the cakes sitting in the car, licked the cream off my fingers, and then drove to the restaurant where I was meeting Hal. He had chosen the location: Big Shuggie's Fish 'n' Chippy. I hoped I was dressed smartly enough for it.

I soon found out. At the front of the restaurant was the kitchen—well, when I say kitchen, I mean two deep-fat fryers from which emanated the mouth-watering aroma of deep-fried everything. Behind the counter stood a man who I can only assume was Big Shuggie himself. He was enormous. He looked as though he could have eaten the contents of all the steaming fryers in front of him, and still had room for one of the fryers itself. He had a long greying ponytail which was pulled back tightly from his face, giving him an instant facelift. I would have to try that. A cigarette dangled from his mouth. I watched as ash fell off the cigarette end and dropped into the fish fryer. I made a mental note to steer clear of the crispy cod.

The other half of the room contained four booths with faded red plastic seats and battered and chipped red Formica tables. The 'battered and chipped' might have been irony, since we were in a fish and chip shop, but I suspect it was just old age. At one of the tables two elderly gents silently tucked into heaped plates of deep-fried fish, chips and mushy peas. Two tables were empty and at the back sat a short, skinny man, with a face like a smug rat. He looked to be in his mid-fifties. The four hairs on top of his head were greased down into one of those comb-overs that always look so strange at rest, and even stranger when the wind blows. By contrast, his nose and ears were sprouting bushy wads of hair. It was as though someone had reached into his nose and ear cavities, got hold of the roots of his hair from the inside and pulled really hard. His grey suit was so shiny that I was amazed he hadn't slid off the red plastic seating, and he was wearing a matching grey shirt that I would have been willing to bet had once been white. Some time in the late 1940s probably. In fact, the whole outfit looked as though it could well have been his demob suit.

I took out my printout of the Perfect Match confirmation e-mail, with the details of my ideal man. Obviously, the extremely handsome, fit, blue-eyed 32-year-old, 6'3" millionaire businessman with all his own hair and teeth, too romantic for his own good, sensitive, caring, and fond of children, was running a tad late. There was no-one in here yet who looked as though his hobbies included going to the gym, skiing, eating out, commitment, long walks on the beach and cosy nights at home in front of roaring fires.

Smug Rat-Faced Man looked at me as I approached, so I smiled politely and sat down at the adjoining table next to the window so I could look out and see my hero arriving in his Bentley, driven by his chauffeur Jeeves. We would probably adjourn to the comfy Bentley later and get jiggy with it on the soft beige leather seats while drinking champagne and feeding each other caviar with a tiny silver spoon, as Jeeves drove us around Hal Litosis' country estate, politely ignoring the sounds of rampant sex from the back seat.

I was rather peeved when Smug Rat-Faced Man disturbed my fantasies, just as Hal and I were getting to the good bit, by easing himself onto the red plastic seat opposite me.

"I'm terribly sorry," I said. "I'm waiting for my date."

"If you're Helena Handbasket, then hubba hubba, your luck's in, lass. Hal Litosis is the name, charmin' the ladies is the game."

At first, his words didn't register in my mind, I was too busy looking at his mouth.

It looked as though he had recently paid a visit to the False Teeth Shop but was obviously in a great hurry on teeth shopping day. I knew this because he had the most perfect set of top teeth (apart from the fact that they moved independently from his gums) but he only had two yellow bottom teeth (and I don't mean he had two yellow bottom teeth in an otherwise perfect set. I mean he had only two bottom teeth, and they were bright yellow). Watching him speak was like watching a badly dubbed Hungarian film. When he finished speaking, his top teeth were still in motion—moving away from his gums, out over his bottom lip, and on a couple of really scary occasions they were sucked back into his mouth and disappeared towards his throat. I was mentally practising the Heimlich manoeuvre, just in case he got over-excited and swallowed them.

It was only then that the actual words sank in. "You're Hal Litosis?" I squealed.

"Aye, lass." He leaned back in his seat and grinned lasciviously at me, using his forefinger to rootle about in his nose. His curious finger disappeared so far up his nostril that I hoped he wasn't looking for his birth certificate to prove his identity. He took out his finger and inspected it. I, on the other hand, looked for a hole of swallow-me-up size. "I'm Hal Litosis. And if you play your cards right, you could be Mrs Litosis within a matter of weeks."

I must have looked shocked at the thought (I was going for horrified but he may not have caught the nuance) because he said, "Aye, lass, as you get to know me you'll realise that I'm a plain-speaking man. I say what I like and I like what I bloody well say. I'm a self-made man and I believe in plain hard work, plain speaking, plain food, plain sex and a good plain woman wi' a bit o' meat on her. You'll do for me, lass. Let's not fanny about. Neither of us have got time on our side. You've got childbearing hips but not much time left to use them. What do ye say?"

I didn't quite know what to say. I settled for, "Shall we have lunch?"

"Good idea, lass. Now, I'm in a good mood, so pick anything from the menu as long as it's under four pounds fifty."

I needed a good helping of fat and sugar to calm my nerves, so I chose a deep-fried Snickers Bar and a cup of tea, while my date plumped for "a nice fat sausage, if you know what I mean."

As we waited for the food, I hazarded an attempt at conversation. "You're nothing like your description on the Perfect Match website, Mr Litosis."

He looked at me with one eye, the other roaming the restaurant for I knew not what. "Aye, well, you weren't exactly truthful yourself, lass." He pulled out a sheet of paper and read it: "'Slim, mid-twenties, natural redhead . . .' You might have been slim at some point but it was probably as long ago as you last saw your mid-twenties. And if that hair's naturally red . . . well . . . then I'm a monkey's uncle." This, I thought was more than likely. "Let's face it, lass, neither of us will ever see forty again will we?"

"I'm thirty-five!" I said.

He raised his eyebrows, but the food arrived just then so he didn't say anything.

Watching him eat was almost as awe-inspiring as watching him talk. It almost put me off my deep-fried Snickers. In the end, I just averted my eyes. I had no idea false teeth could do all that.

"So, lass, what work do you do?" Hal delicately patted his mouth with his shirttail and burped in a satisfied way.

"I'm a private detective."

"A private dick? A shamus? A gumshoe?"

I nodded. Maybe I should introduce him to Fifi if things didn't work out between us. They could trade hardboiled slang.

"By heck, lass, that's no job for a lady. You'll have to give that up when we're wed. You can take over care of the pigs back home."

"Oh, are you a farmer, Hal?"

"Nay, lass, I just have a couple of dozen pigs. Good eatin' when they're dead and good company while they're alive."

I shuddered, not wanting to dwell on that one too much. "So, what is it you do?" I took a sip of my tea.

"I'm Human Resources Manager at Stubezzi Industries. By heck, lass . . . no need to spit your tea at me. If tha wants to trade body fluids I can think of a much better way. An' it doesn't involve me havin' to get my suit cleaned." He paused thoughtfully. "Well, it might do . . . it's been a long time, I might be a bit . . . keen, if you know what I mean."

I thought it was safer, and by far less nauseating, to concentrate on the first part of what he had said. "You work at Stubezzi Industries?" What an amazing coincidence. Who would have thought it?

"Aye, lass. I'm Evan Stubezzi's right-hand man. I have files on everyone and everything at that place, believe me."

I thought quickly. Maybe this date wouldn't turn out to be such a washout after all. "Oh Hal, I'd love to see your office. Would you take me to see it?"

He looked puzzled. "My office? Wouldn't you rather see my bedroom? I changed the sheets at the beginning of August and I've got a couple of bottles of Pale Ale on ice." August? Today was October 8th. "I thought we could go back for a bit of 'Hows-Your-Father' so I could give you a trial run, like. See if we were compatible in the sack."

I wasn't flattered. It felt as though I had been compared to the pigs and found wanting. "Oh, but I'd love to see your office. I get really . . . hot . . . in the offices of important men in Human Resources. If you know what I mean." I was almost making myself vomit, but a job's a job. I had to get in and see those files. And it was a language he understood.

"By heck, lass. You're a feisty little minx and that's for sure. I'll have you over that table and your drawers off quicker than you can say 'Pig in a poke'. Come on, drink up, let's go." He stood up, dragging me by the arm and flinging a ten-pound note down on the table. He didn't even wait for the change.

He pulled me outside.

"Um, would you like a lift?" I asked.

"Nay, lass, you follow me. I've got my wheels here." He pointed to a rust-coloured 1984 Skoda. Well, probably just 'rust' would be more accurate.

"I thought you were a millionaire."

"Near enough, near enough. But I'm not one for these fancy cars and houses. I don't waste my hard-earned cash on frivolities like clothes and cars and fancy restaurants and central heating. I'm saving my money for a bit of luxury in our old age—a few chickens, a new fridge every twenty years or so, and maybe a week at a caravan park in Skegness every summer. This car's done me proud and will see me through a few more years yet." He untied the string that held the door—if not the whole car—together, and switched on the engine. He had to shout to be heard over the exhaust, which had more holes in it than a used teabag poked full of extra holes for the hell of it. "Follow me, and if you get lost, we're going to Stubezzi Industries at The Stubezzi Building, number 15 Valley Forge Business Park."

A-ha—the very same address that Emma Roids had given me. Isn't it fascinating how you can go all that time without hearing the name Evan Stubezzi and then it turns up on everybody's lips, everybody seems to work there, and the name is linked in some way to three serial murders? Maybe I would discover that the serial killer was Evan Stubezzi himself. Or would that be too much of a coincidence? I started my car and set off behind Hal. I didn't switch the GPS on. The chances of me losing a 20-year-old Skoda were slim to nil.

When I lost Hal's Skoda, I pulled into the side of the road and asked directions from a passing schoolboy. Hal was waiting for me in the car park when I arrived. Stubezzi Industries was an enormous concrete and glass building, with a fountain and a bizarre modern art statue (that looked like a squirrel vomiting into a toilet) looming over the concourse in front of the building. The cavernous reception area had a marble floor, lots of brass and plants and two maroon-suited commissionaires standing stiffly behind an impressive semi-circular desk. Behind them were banks of closed circuit televisions, above which a computerised screen flashed through the various companies that made up Stubezzi Industries:

Stubezzi Electronics—with an accompanying picture of DVD players, computers and stereos.
Stubezzi Fashions—a pair of models wearing evening dress.
Stubezzi Gems—a glittering heap of precious stones.
Stubezzi Cold Storage—pictures of sides of beef hanging in a big warehouse.
Stubezzi Import/Export—for which there was no accompanying picture, just the tag line 'No, we don't know what it means either, and we don't talk about it very much.'

Hal nodded at the two commissionaires. "Hey-up, lads. I'm just taking my fiancée up for a quick rogering over the conference table. The boss in?"

One of the commissionaires shook his head. "Nah, Hal. He's not been in for a few days. Last time I saw him he was out buying a dark suit and a pair of sunglasses, but his secretary, Emma Roids, is in. Give your fiancée one from me, by the way."

Hal pushed me into the lift before I could protest. How rude of the commissionaire, getting someone else to do his dirty work for him. He could give me one himself if he was so keen.

"I thought Emma Roids was Justin Case's secretary?" I said as the lift ascended.

"She was, but she got promoted when Justin were murdered."

The doors opened at the sixth floor.

I wondered whether Emma Roids' promotion was significant, but it was probably totally irrelevant. We walked down a quiet corridor lined in oak panels and covered in a thick maroon carpet. My feet sank into the luxurious pile. As Hal ushered me to his office he explained that this was the executive floor. No doubt the other floors had much less luxurious surroundings.

Hal's office was about four times the size of mine and had more furniture than my whole house did. Dominating the room was a huge desk, covered with paper and files. Hal locked the door, knocked the files off the desk with a masterful sweep of the arm, and said, "Now then, lass, get tha's kit off and let the dog see the rabbit."

I thought quickly. "Oh Hal, just give me a few moments to prepare myself. How about a little drinkie before we start?"

Hal pulled open a drawer. "I think I've got a carton of milk somewhere. Not sure how fresh it is though."

"No, silly. I mean a real drink." I sat down on the desk and crossed my legs. "Surely there must be a drinks cabinet somewhere around. Maybe in Mr Stubezzi's office? Why don't you go and have a look and I'll . . . change into something more comfortable . . . like . . . like a post-it note and a couple of paperclips."

"Right, lass. Will do." He chucked me under the chin. "Keep it warm 'til I come back. And remind me to take my teeth out before we get stuck in." I fought back a wave of nausea and smiled bravely.

With a lecherous wink he unlocked the door and I watched him strutting his funky stuff down the corridor like a 70's disco god. "Doo-doo-doo-doo-doo-doo-doo-doo-doo. Like a sex machine. Yeah baby." His knock knees and clenched buttocks were not so much *Saturday Night Fever* as *Sunday Morning Diarrhoea*.

I rushed to the door and locked it behind him and then went over to the filing cabinet and started opening drawers and flicking through files. I learned some very interesting things from those files. Luke Warmwater had indeed worked at Stubezzi Import/Export as Purchasing Manager, but had been fired just over a month ago, apparently after getting into a fight with Evan Stubezzi. It was also clear that numerous complaints had been made about Emma Roids' snooping and spying, but that the complaints had suddenly been withdrawn. In a flash of completely unexplained and unexplainable inspiration, I wondered whether Emma Roids had found something out about them and decided to blackmail them. Was that why they had withdrawn their complaints? Two of the names of the original complainants were familiar to me: Justin Case and Luke Warmwater.

I recognised their names because they were both dead—one of those spooky coincidences that kept cropping up in this case. A couple of the names were unfamiliar—Wayne Kerr, Marketing Manager, and Jacqueline Hyde, Publicity. I made a note to go and see them at some point if I had nothing better to do. And I also thought it might be useful to speak to the taciturn Emma again.

I also learned something else which was very, very interesting, but I'm going to keep that one to myself a little longer.

I could hear Hal coming back along the corridor singing, "I'm so sexy it huuuuuurts" so I hurriedly thrust the files back into the drawers, picked up my handbag, and unlocked the door, slipping out before Hal could cut off my escape route.

"Hal, baby, I'm really sorry. I just got a message on my pager thing. It was . . . ummm . . . the Mother Superior at the local convent. She was ringing to tell me that one of the nuns has suddenly dropped out of the . . . errr . . . nun course and so a place has suddenly opened up for me. I'm so sorry. I was really looking forward to our little tryst. But this whole nun thing is a childhood dream and means that I have to take a vow of celibacy." I shrugged. "*C'est la vie* and all that."

Hal stood there for a minute, open-mouthed, with a pathetic expression on his face. Then he sucked his teeth back into position. "Can you not tell 'em you'll start tomorrow? You'll have a lifetime of celibacy. You might as well have a night to remember."

"I'm sorry, Hal, but when God calls . . ." I tried to look holy and angelic, which, if I remembered it correctly from the pictures at Sunday School when I was little, was something akin to looking constipated.

"Oh well, lass, if that's your decision . . ."

"Bless you, Hal, you're an understanding man." I moved his strand of hair aside and kissed him on top of his little pink head. "I'll make sure there's a nice little freeholding for you in Heaven, with some lovely plump pigs."

"Thanks, lass." He sighed, a hangdog expression on his weaselly little face, before suddenly brightening up. "I suppose I'd better have another look through the details of the other birds Perfect Match supplied me with." He pointed to his crotch. "Don't want all this perfect luvin' to go to waste, after all."

"That's the spirit, Hal."

I strode off down the corridor, leaving Hal behind me mumbling, "Well, that were a right bloody waste of four fifty."

Since I was already in the building, and so many things seemed to come back to Evan Stubezzi and his missing diamonds, I decided to snoop a little bit. The executive floor seemed like the place to start. I waited until Hal had gone back into his room and then doubled back to check out Evan Stubezzi's office. This turned out to be a whole suite, complete with living room, bathroom and bedroom, as well as the most magnificent desk I have ever seen. The anteroom looked to be his secretary's office and, although I could see evidence that someone had been there earlier today, and the computer was on, there was no sign of Emma Roids.

I sat down at the computer. In front of me was a screen with a picture of Emma's two dogs, sitting in a fur-lined basket, looking every inch the pampered pooches they were. Down at the bottom of the screen was a row of little graphic images, each of which looked for all the world like a little piece of paper with a big 'W' scrawled on it. Each of them had a name: 'work', 'dogs', 'accounts', 'blackmail', 'shopping'. I'd seen this type of computery thing before.

I took out my cell phone and called Heidi. I quietly explained to her what I had in front of me and asked her what I needed to do.

"Double click on the *document* you want to see." Document, huh? I double-clicked and it worked. The girl was a computer genius. I was constantly amazed at all the arcane stuff she knew.

The documents turned out to be reminders of things Emma needed to do in the various compartments of her life—take the dogs to the beauty parlour, go to the bank and deposit a 'b.mail payment' (whatever that was), type some contracts for Stubezzi, book a holiday in the Maldives. Strangely enough, though, the most interesting document was the one labelled 'blackmail'. This gave a list of names, dates and amounts of money. The names were the ones I had already seen: Justin Case, Luke Warmwater, Jacqueline Hyde and Wayne Kerr. The amounts were steady: Justin Case £1500pm, Luke Warmwater £1000pm, Jacqueline Hyde £1250pm and Wayne Kerr £1500pm. A note at the bottom of the document read: 'Case and Warmwater dead. Find new victims??? (Stubezzi or Litosis, perhaps?) Incr. payments for Hyde and Kerr??? Police??'

I wasn't sure what it meant, but I had a bad feeling about it all. I closed the document and decided to look around the rest of Stubezzi's opulent suite.

I found Emma Roids in the bathroom, giving Ruby and Emerald a bath. They apparently went everywhere with her. I couldn't tell which was which as their little bows and diamante collars were sitting on the shelf. It didn't matter. Both of them growled at me anyway. Emma scooped them up. "Oh my poor babies. Is the nasty lady back to ask mummy horrid questions again?" She wrapped them in a thick towel and dried them off. I picked up Ruby's little red bow and started to twist it around my finger.

"Emma, can I ask you some questions?"

She snatched the bow off me, and picked the dogs' trinkets off the shelf.

"No. I'm not telling you about my blackmail scam so don't think you can drag it out of me with your sneaky questions."

"It's not—"

"Look, I'm not going to tell you why I was blackmailing that chiselling bastard Justin Case for fifteen hundred per month. I know that he was embezzling from Evan Stubezzi and I threatened to tell Stubezzi. Case was petrified. Stubezzi is a hard cold man and you wouldn't want to cross him."

"Were you—?"

"Oh my God, you're so brutal, forcing me to answer. I'm not going to tell you. You can't make me tell you that I was blackmailing Luke Warmwater too, because he had been stealing from the warehouse for the last ten years and that he also helped Robin and Owen Banks with the jewel heist. The fact that I've known about it all along and had been blackmailing Warmwater for the last eight years is just none of your business."

"I don't—"

"Yes, they're both gone now, but don't make me tell you about my other victims. I don't have any other victims and if I did they wouldn't be called Jacqueline Hyde and Wayne Kerr."

"I'm sorry—"

"Oh, you can't make me tell you why I'm blackmailing them, you cruel bitch. OK, OK, you're killing me here with your endless, endless questions. Wayne Kerr used to be called Jayne and Jacqueline Hyde had a baby out of wedlock in her teens."

"If you—"

"Dear merciful heavens, leave me alone. No, I'm not telling you that the baby turned out to be Evan Stubezzi. That is absolutely not true. And if you dare spread that around I'll kill you."

I finally managed to get my question out. "Miss Roids, where do you get your hair done?"

"I can't take it any more. Please, no more questions." She covered her face with her hands. The dogs at her feet yapped at me accusingly. I didn't exactly kick them—more like just nudged them with my toe.

"Oh, well then, I just thought I'd ask." I shrugged and turned to leave the room. I knew I was never going to get any information out of her. She was the most closed-mouthed person I had ever met.

She grabbed me tightly by the arm, her fingernails digging into my skin. I looked at her face. Her eyes had become hard and cold and she put her face up close to mine and hissed, "Remember, Helena, everyone has secrets and everyone has a price." I was intrigued. It was a special skill to be able to hiss a whole sentence—especially one with so few sibilants.

"Well, thanks for your time Emma. I'd love to stop and chat a bit longer, but I have four murders to investigate and some stolen jewels to find, and I don't seem to be getting very far."

I left the office and walked back along the corridor. As I passed Hal's office again, I paused. I heard him inside, talking on the phone.

"Well, lass, you sound like a foxy mare and no mistake. Fancy meeting up for a bit of hanky panky later? Play your cards right and I'll even treat you to a pint and a pickled egg at the Working Men's Club after I've had me wicked way with you." It sounded as though he'd bounced back from his earlier disappointment. I was glad. Despite the fact that we obviously weren't compatible, and I would probably have nightmares about his false teeth for the rest of my life, I rather liked Hal.

I decided to check out the offices at the other end of the corridor. I listened at each door as I passed and opened a couple of them out of interest. The offices inside were similar to Hal's in size and grandeur. At the far end of the hallway, the nameplate on the last office caught my eye: 'Jacqueline Hyde—Publicity'. Inside, I heard muffled sobs. I tapped gently on the door. There was no answer but the sobbing stopped. I tapped again and then turned the handle. A tiny elderly lady sat at the desk. Her eyes were red and the tip of her nose was shiny. Tears streaked through the thick pale powder on her cheeks, giving her face a rather blotched appearance.

"Oh dear, I must look a terrible state." She sniffed and reached into a large brown leather handbag and pulled out an antique mother-of-pearl powder compact. It was beautiful, studded with tiny diamonds, one or two of which were missing. She saw me looking at it and handed it to me. "It was my mother's. But I'll probably have to sell it soon, too." With the 'too' she burst into fresh tears.

"Whatever's the matter?"

She pulled herself together again. "All sorts of things, dear, but I'm sure everything will work out. Now, what can I do for you?"

I hadn't really thought about what I was going to say. "I'm a friend of Hal's and was just visiting."

"But you still have your clothes on. If you managed to get out of his office with your virtue intact then I'm impressed at your ingenuity, my dear." Her eyes twinkled. "I never manage to get out unscathed." The crafty old goat. My estimation of Hal went up still further.

"I was just having a look around. It's a lovely office building. Have you worked here long?"

"About forty years." She sighed. "It used to be a wonderful honest place to work, but things have changed rather since old Mr Stubezzi retired and his son Evan took over." Her lips quivered. "I don't think I'll be here much longer, especially now . . ." Her voice trailed off and her eyes filled up again.

Suddenly, things fell into place. "You mean, since Emma Roids became his secretary?"

Her distress increased. "Miss Roids is *not* a nice young lady. She has a nasty habit of worming secrets out of people and then using those secrets against them."

"Is she blackmailing you, Jacqueline?" It's not for nothing that I'm a private investigator. Sometimes I can actually be quite bright.

She nodded. "Please don't make me tell you why. And now she's increased the payments. And I just don't know how I'm going to manage."

I thought back to the note on Emma Roids' computer. The increases had been mentioned, but Emma was obviously worried about the police finding out, if her final notation was anything to go by. And maybe I could make that happen. I stood up. "Don't worry about it. Leave it with me and I'll see what I can do."

Jacqueline smiled weakly at me. "You're very kind dear, but please don't go to any bother over me. Oh, and dear?"

"Yes?"

"I hope you don't mind me saying so, but that outfit is ever so slightly slutty."

"You think?" Excellent—the very look I had been going for. It was good to know.

X,X,X,X,X,

I drove back home to feed Virgil and decide what to do next. As I put the key in the door the phone started ringing, so I dashed inside and picked up the receiver. It was my mum. I hadn't spoken to her for a couple of days and, true to form, she took this as a sign that I was lying drunk in an alleyway, had been murdered in my bed, or had been kidnapped by aliens or madmen. I knew I would have to be careful about what I said regarding my latest case, and the fact that my next-door neighbour had been both mad *and* murdered. And I *definitely* couldn't tell her that I was trawling for dates on the internet—or the 'microwave', as she called it. Luckily, I didn't actually have to speak as she launched into a long and complicated story about my Dad and a contretemps with a garden gnome, before telling me the latest successes of my siblings. I bore it in silence, my teeth gritted. She called us collectively: 'My daughter the dentist, my son the headmaster, and poor dear Helena,' a phrase always accompanied by raised eyebrows, as though indicating that I was locked up in the attic, Mrs Rochester-like, for everyone's safety. While she was speaking I suddenly noticed that everything was not as I had left it earlier that day. Drawers were lying on the floor, cupboards were open, and the contents were scattered everywhere. My sofa cushions were lying in a heap and furniture had been moved into the centre of the room. Either I had a particularly messy poltergeist, or I had been burgled.

"Mum," I broke in, "I'm sorry, but I have to go."

"Fine, dear, but have a think about what I said about getting a proper job and losing a few pounds, will you? I'd hate you to be a fat and lonely old maid with a dead-end job when your dad and I aren't here any more to look after you."

"Yep. Will do. Bye for now." I put the phone down and looked around at the devastation that was my living room. I wondered what the burglars had taken. Nothing appeared to be missing downstairs. Upstairs, the panel had been pulled off the side of the bath but the two bedrooms appeared more or less undisturbed. Maybe the burglar had been put off when he opened my underwear drawer. I should keep a drawer of skimpy silken underthings for just such an occasion and hide my comfortable plain cotton granny knickers away out of sight. How embarrassing. Then I noticed that the mattress of my bed was at an angle. I checked underneath. The samurai sword and the note that Detective Lee had asked me to keep safe were gone. How unfortunate that a burglar should visit me just when I was holding some important evidence for the police. Bloody typical.

I went back downstairs and made two phone calls. One was to Fifi (everything was jake, from hell to breakfast; she'd stocked up on my eel juice; she'd got herself a gat from some chiselling boob in a game of rats and mice; and did I want her to fill anyone full of daylight and fit them for a wooden kimono? To which I replied: good, thanks, lovely and not right now, and hoped that those were the right responses). The scary sisters had been on the blower again, issuing more threats, but Fifi had apparently confused the hell out of them by calling them tomatoes and asking them to cut her a huzz, so they said they'd call back when someone who spoke English was in. I told Fifi that I would be in the office later, but that she could take the rest of the afternoon off. The other call was to Frank Lee. I didn't want to tell him about the burglary over the phone and I also thought it was about time I filled him in on some of the things I'd uncovered, so I said I was coming down to the police station and wanted to speak to him and Agent Art Ifarti. I needed to tell Frank what was going on, and I needed to find out who Agent Ifarti really was.

The field of eligible men was getting worryingly narrow. Owen Banks was possibly a serial womaniser who was particularly careless of both girlfriends and cars, Detective Lee didn't appear to like me very much, Art Ifarti was still a possible but it would be nice to find out his real name before committing myself, and Hal Litosis was definitely not boyfriend material. I'd read that, statistically, over the age of thirty the chances of a woman finding a partner reduce by five percent a year. The serial killer wasn't helping matters either. He'd reduced the field even further in the space of a couple of days—OK, one of his victims was married, one was bonkers, one was a petty thief with a David Beckham fixation and one was a jewel thief in hiding—but, still.

CHAPTER FIFTEEN

(When You Run Out Of Plot, Just Have Someone
Come Through The Door Waving A Gun)

The nice policeman on the desk was getting used to me now. He buzzed me through, handing me a donut as I passed. "You're going to need one of these if you want to look as though you fit in."

Frank and Art were waiting for me in the Incident Room, glowering at each other.

"Did you bring the evidence?" Frank asked. "The sword and the note?"

"Well, not exactly."

"They might as well be at your place as anywhere else. They'd probably just go missing from our evidence room anyway. And the Lab has a backlog at the moment, so they wouldn't be able to get round to running their tests. Just make sure you keep them safe. We wouldn't want the samurai sword to get back into the hands of the serial killer, would we?"

"Oh, I'm sure it's safe."

"Well, let's . . . what do you mean, 'you're sure it's safe'? Don't you know where it is?"

"Ummm . . . I know where it *isn't*, if that's any help. It's not under my mattress any longer."

Until that moment, I'd never actually understood the term 'go ballistic'. If the fusillade of cursing hadn't been directed at *me*, I would have found it interesting and fun to watch. As it was, I wanted to cower in a trench until the attack was over. Art Ifarti sat through it all with an amused look on his face, throwing me a conspiratorial wink from time to time.

Once Frank was winding down I said, "Anyway, let's not cry over stolen evidence. Let me tell you what I've found out."

I filled them in on everything I'd learned so far. Well, almost everything. I told them that I was sure the murders were connected to Evan Stubezzi and the diamond heist five years ago. Both of them pooh-poohed that idea.

"It's true," I insisted. "And I even know where the diamonds are, so there." That part wasn't exactly true, but you know how it is when you're trying to impress people and they scoff at you. You exaggerate things a bit, you stretch the truth, and sometimes you outright lie. Saying that I knew where the diamonds were was door C—an outright lie, but I was adamant. It worked. They were well impressed and listened to me more carefully from then on.

I told them that three of the victims were directly linked to Evan Stubezzi—either through the jewel heist, or being his employees—and that my neighbour, Jerry Mander, had obviously known something that the killer wouldn't have wanted publicised.

"I wouldn't be surprised if the serial killer is Evan Stubezzi."

"Don't be stupid." Lee and I looked at Ifarti. His normal, laid-back facade had cracked for a moment. Ifarti shrugged. "He's a businessman, an important figure in the community. I've heard he's a real nice guy."

"He runs an Import/Export agency—and you know what that means," I said. They both looked at me expectantly. "You know—drugs, prostitutes, money laundering."

Ifarti snorted. "That's ridiculous. Import/Export is a perfectly fine legitimate business. Why, I . . . I have a brother in Import/Export." He tailed off.

"So, what does he do exactly?"

"Well, he imports and exports stuff."

"There. I rest my case," I said.

I also told them my theory about Emma Roids and her blackmailing scam. Of course, I didn't have any proof of this, and it had been impossible to get any information from Emma herself, but I thought it was worth mentioning.

Now it was my turn to extract some information. "So, Art, what part of America is it you're from?"

"Alabama, honey," he drawled.

"Really, what town in Alabama? I have an aunt in Alabama. Perhaps you know her?"

"Oh, I doubt it, honey. I come from New York City, Alabama. It's a mighty big place."

"New York's in the south of Alabama? Is that right?"

"Sure is, y'all. The Big Apple. The City that never sleeps. My kind of town. Ah, Manhattan, Broadway, The Bronx, the Hudson River . . ." His eyes clouded over as he reminisced about his home town.

"What body of water is it that the Hudson flows into again?"

"The good old Mississippi River. My lord, I love that big muddy ole river."

"My aunt is the coroner of New York City, Alabama. You've probably heard of her? Kay Scarletta?"

"Why of course I know Kay—everyone knows Kay—she's just the best goddam scuba diving, cordon bleu chef, pathologist we have, is all, y'all."

That settled it. He was telling the truth.

I'd have to tell Heidi that the computer was wrong. It must have a virus or something. Art was back on my list of eligible men. OK, it was a fairly short list: Ifarti and Lee, with careless, carless lothario Owen Banks on the subs bench. I hadn't so much narrowed the list down, as the other candidates had been eliminated from my enquiries, so to speak.

I picked up my bag. "OK, guys. I'm going to nip to the office before going home. And I really must go grocery shopping and charge up my phone. And sleep. Sleep would be good. Also I need to bandage the gunshot wound Jerry Mander gave me, re-bandage my other wounds and rest my dislocated shoulder and knee, broken ribs, arm, fractured jaw, etcetera, etcetera. Bet you'd forgotten about those, hadn't you?"

Ifarti tried again. "Aren't you going to tell us where these little old diamonds are, honey?"

"The dia . . .? Oh yes, the diamonds. Don't worry. They're in a very safe place." I hoped they were in a safer place than under a mattress somewhere. That was obviously a hiding place that burglars had cottoned on to. Who'd have guessed they were so smart?

Lee showed me out to my car. As I was about to climb in, he took my arm. "Helena, watch out for Ifarti. I get the impression he's not all he seems."

"Oh, don't worry about me, Frank." It seemed we were on first name terms again. "I'm perfectly capable of looking after myself."

He shrugged. "OK, Handbasket, but don't come running to me when you next get your legs dislocated. I wouldn't like to have to say, 'I told you so'."

It looked as though first name terms were off the menu again. I'd never known anyone who ran so hot and cold as Lee.

XXXXX

I drove to the office with Franz Ferdinand's 'Shopping For Blood' on the CD player and parked outside. Fifi had taken me at my word and had gone for the day, although she'd left me a note that read: 'Boss, everything's silk so far, so I'm dusting. Off to tie a bag on with a zazoo. All wool and a yard wide. Plant ya now, dig ya later, dollface.' After some thought, I took this to mean that everything was OK, so she was leaving to go for a drink with some snappy dresser and that she was really looking forward to it. Hey, I was finally getting the hang of this hardboiled lingo. Or was I? Was a zazoo something like a yak?

I locked the door—I was too busy for visitors—and took the phone off the hook.

I switched all my new machines on, which took me about ten minutes. Fifi had bought some new shelves and arranged everything neatly. I wished I could remember what all the machines did. I'd have to get Heidi to show me again. And this time I would take notes.

I sat in front of the computer and fired off a stroppy e-mail to Perfect Match, telling them they should vet their applicants before sending them on dates. OK, I had stretched the truth a little bit as far as my age and real hair colour were concerned, but not as far as Hal, who had described himself as 'Handsome Young Millionaire'. I looked at the other potential dates Perfect Match had provided me with. Could I trust that 'Actor', 'Male Model', 'Rock Star' and 'Sex God' were really as they had described themselves? Especially 'Sex God'. I would be particularly gutted if he turned out to be a figment of his own fevered imagination.

I started to type up my notes from the case, getting engrossed with the detail. All of a sudden, I felt the hairs on the back of my neck stand on end. It felt as though I was being watched. We're extraordinarily sensitive and prescient, us private detectives. Our senses are keen. We feel things way before they happen, and we have the reactions of mongooses. Or is that mongeese? Anyway, it's a gift, and not always a welcome one, but we suffer it, because of our overriding ambition to help people and right the wrongs done in the name of greed and hate. I guess you could say we're sort of superheroes—only without the cloaks and the tights. Oh, and we can't fly or climb up the side of buildings without the aid of a rope. My eyesight and hearing is acute, and I pride myself that I can hear the softest footfall from five hundred yards away, and feel the presence of someone before they're anywhere near me. So, when I had the feeling that I was being watched, I took it seriously.

I looked up. Aurora deGreasepaint and Smilla da\
standing in front of my desk. I was looking down the ba\
It was . . . ooooh, one of those big black ones that needs t\
hold. The two hands belonged to Smilla.

"The door was locked," I said. "How the hell did you . . .?"

Aurora stepped to one side so that I could see the door. Th\
a fist-sized hole in the glass, just above the lock, and pieces c
on the floor. How had I not heard the glass smashing? The glazic
going to be rubbing his hands with glee by the end of this case. M\
glass was not such a good idea. Perhaps I should just have a p\
wooden door. But I liked the tradition. I liked the idea that someo\
outside, in need of help, could walk up the stairs and see my pacing
fedora-topped shadow through the frosted glass of my office door. Of
course, I didn't actually have a fedora, but take it from me, a soup bowl
looks remarkably like one when seen through frosted glass.

"Ladies," I said, nodding at each of them in turn. "How lovely to see
you again. May I ask to what I owe this pleasure?"

"We told you to keep your big nose out."

There was Aurora with the nasal insults again. If I wasn't so well-
balanced I could end up with a complex from all this and really start to
believe that my nose was not of normal, or at most slightly larger than
normal, size.

Smilla nodded and twitched the gun menacingly towards my big
nose; apparently such a huge target that even an elderly blind mole
which had lost its sense of smell could find it in the dark with its paws
tied behind its back.

"We politely asked you to stay away from Robin and Owen Banks, to
forget about the diamonds, and to forget you'd ever heard of us. And
did you do that? Did you?"

"Not exactly. I—"

"Shut up."

"If you're going to ask rhetorical questions I wish you'd make it a
little clearer. Maybe Smilla could give me a slight nod if I'm supposed
to answer. It seems jolly unfair if you get all the good dialogue and all
she gets to do is hold the gun steady."

Smilla raised her eyebrows. Roughly translated I took this to mean:
"Can I shoot the mouthy bitch now, Sis?" because Aurora shook her
head and put a hand on the barrel of the big black gun in a calming
way.

"You think you're so damn smart, don't you?"

"Well, you know," I said, modestly. "Not overly smart, but yes, pretty smart, I suppose. Thanks. Of course, it all depends on your definition of 'smart'. If you're talking book learning and exams and such, then—"

"Shut the fuck up." Aurora and I both looked at Smilla. She shrugged. "Well, she's so bloody annoying."

Aurora took back the reins as speaker again. "Anyway, we want you to drop this case. And this is the last time we ask you nicely."

"You call this nicely? This is the second time you've come into my office, broken the glass in my door, threatened me—"

Smilla cocked the gun.

"OK, it's the first time you've actually brought a gun along. So you're turning up the heat a bit. But why should I give up this case? What's it to you?" Why had I left my gun at home that morning?

"That's really none of your business, as I think I've explained before." Aurora placed both hands flat on the desk and leaned closer. "Now. Just. Butt. Out. Is that quite clear?"

"Actually, no. I'm getting pretty pissed off with being ordered about by you two without a by your leave or a reason, as it happens." Behind the two sisters, through what was left of the frosted glass of the door, I could see a shadow moving on the landing. The handle started to turn slowly and I raised my voice to cover the sound of the door opening. "All you've done since the first time you showed your faces here is insult me, threaten me, and tell me not to do stuff. I haven't had to put up with behaviour like that since I left home. So just bugger off and stop pointing guns at me."

"And what if we don't?" Aurora glanced at Smilla. "Aim low. Give her a warning shot." I shut my eyes.

A shot rang out and I flinched. I was hit. Oh my God, I was bleeding. I was going to die a spinster. But why wasn't it hurting? I slowly opened my eyes. Smilla was clutching her arm and groaning. The gun was lying on the floor between Smilla and Aurora, and Aurora was standing transfixed.

"Helena," said Agent Art Ifarti, "just kick the gun towards me." He stood at the door, looking handsome and rakish with a smoking pistol in his right hand.

"No!" said Aurora. "Don't do it. He'll kill us all."

I skipped around the side of the desk and kicked Smilla's gun over to Art, who picked it up without taking his eye off Aurora.

"Well, he might kill you two, Aurora, but he won't kill me. After all, I'm on the side of the angels and the FBI never kill the good guys." Art smiled at me. Damn, he did look especially handsome carrying a couple of weapons.

"FBI?" Aurora looked from me to Art.

"Yep. Please allow me to introduce Special Agent Art Ifarti, from good old New York City, Alabama."

She snorted. "He's no FBI agent. God, you're so gullible. First you get taken in by Owen Banks, and now this guy pulls the wool over your eyes. Are you thick, or what?"

"Of course he's an FBI agent. He's been helping the police and me with these serial killings."

Aurora scoffed. "Oh yeah. I'm sure he knows all about the serial killings. Why don't you tell her exactly what you know, Evan?"

"Evan?" I was baffled.

"Sorry, Helena." The agent formerly known as Art Ifarti had mysteriously lost his southern accent. "I'm Evan Stubezzi." He shrugged. "Whoops."

I was gobsmacked. Now I'd have to cross him off the damn eligibility list. On the other hand: did I? "So, Mr Stubezzi, what does your wife think about you impersonating FBI agents?"

"She doesn't know."

Shit. Oh well. You lose some, you lose some more. I picked up the phone. "I'll just call Frank, shall I, Art . . . errr . . . Evan? Tell him we collared us a couple of perps?" I started to dial Frank's direct line.

Evan Stubezzi swung one of the guns round in my direction, while keeping the other one trained on Aurora, who was trying to staunch the bloodflow from Smilla's arm. "Put the phone down."

"We can't take them in on our own, Evan. Well, maybe we can." I put the phone down and grabbed Smilla by the arm that wasn't bleeding. "I'll take this one, you grab the other."

Art, or rather, Evan, continued to hold the guns steady. "Let's just hold it right there until I get some answers, if you don't mind."

Aurora turned on me. "You don't get it even yet, you silly cow, do you?" She stabbed a finger towards Stubezzi. "He's the bad guy."

"But . . . you're the bad guys," I said.

"Just consider us all bad guys, honey," said Stubezzi. "Just playing for different teams."

"This is exceptionally confusing, you know." I sat down on the desk.

"Would anyone like to explain it to me?"

"It all started with my jewels," Stubezzi said. "These two young ladies here," he gestured to Aurora and Smilla, who were glaring at him, "they were the girlfriends of Owen and Robin Banks." So Aurora had been telling the truth, and that cheating scumbag Owen had been lying. "They discovered that the brothers Banks had ripped me off five years ago with the aid of one of my employees, Luke Warmwater. A trifling amount of some thirty million in diamonds. Robin was the one who had hidden the diamonds, and the only one who knew where they were. As far as I was aware, Robin Banks was the only person involved in the robbery—I didn't know about Warmwater at the time. And until a few months ago Banks was in hiding. Then he contacted Owen. At some point they hooked up with this pair, and these nasty double-crossing witches came to me, knowing that I was looking for Robin Banks. And thanks to them, I found Robin. Only someone had got there first. He was the first victim of the serial killer. I think I disturbed the killer when I arrived at the motel Banks was hiding out in because the body was still warm. The hands had been cut off but not taken away. The scarlet fish and the note in the mouth were already in place." He shrugged. "So I kept him on ice for a few days in my cold storage facility, to see what turned up. And then I sent the hands to Owen as a warning. I thought he might know where the jewels were."

"So who killed Robin? And who's been killing the others?" I looked at the sisters. "These two?"

Aurora spluttered. "We most certainly did not. We're just after the jewels. We don't kill people."

"No?" I glared at her. "Your sister was going to shoot me a little while ago. Is that what you call not killing people?"

"She was aiming low." Her tone was defensive.

"Lower than what? Lower than my knees? Lower than an inch above my head? Exactly how much weapons training have you two had?"

Their silence spoke volumes. Amateurs.

I turned back to Stubezzi. "So, if none of you lot is the serial killer, then who is?"

He shrugged. "I don't know. DeGreasepaint and daCrowde came to see me in my office about five weeks ago. They set the whole jewel heist out for me. Someone must have heard the conversation, or found out about it afterwards. I sacked Luke Warmwater when I found out he had been stealing from me over the years. But I don't know why Justin

Case was killed. Perhaps it was just a coincidence that he worked for me." He shrugged again. "Whoever found out about the missing jewels has been a step ahead of me all the way. That's why I pretended to be an FBI Agent, so that I could get an inside track on the investigation. It hasn't helped though. So I was taking a new tack." He looked at me. "You seemed to be stumbling over dead bodies and clues and bumbling around, so I thought I'd follow you when you left the station earlier and see what happened. This time trouble came to you instead of the other way round. I saw these two coming up here so I followed them and hung around outside the door until the time seemed appropriate to interrupt."

Well, this was all very cosy, wasn't it? "So what do we do now? Bugger off and forget any of this ever happened?"

Stubezzi shook his head. "I don't think so, Helena. I can't trust these two and you'll just go running off to Detective Lee. No, what we're going to do is we're all going to go downstairs—very nicely, as if we're a group of friends taking a pleasant ride—and you're all going to get in my car and I'm going to show you around Stubezzi Cold Storage. The plant is closed for the next few days, so we won't be disturbed."

"Not for me, thanks. I'm a vegetarian." It was a complete lie of course, but I thought it was worth a try. After all, my last lie had proved remarkably effective.

Stubezzi gestured with the gun. "OK, ladies (although I use the term in its loosest possible sense), let's go. It will be a bit chilly in there and it will take you a couple of days to die, but there's plenty to eat."

So much for the lie. I had occasionally considered burning and drowning as the two scariest ways to die. Being frozen to death locked in a cold storage unit with some dead cows—and I'm not referring to Aurora and Smilla—had never crossed my mind. It did now, and the thought was not appealing. I had to be brave and clever and think of something constructive.

"Please don't kill me," I sobbed, throwing myself at the feet of Evan Stubezzi. "I promise I'll never tell anyone, really I won't." I beat my feet and fists on the floor of the office, scaring up a little cloud of dust. I would need to speak to Fifi about getting a cleaner in. All the bad guys looked at me, horrified. "I don't want to die. Don't freeze me to death, please. I don't want to be chopped into bits and hung up on meat hooks."

Just then, the door to the office opened. "Grab a cloud ya torpedoes or I'll squirt metal and fill ya so full of holes yous could double as a tea-bag. I've got plenty of swift so don't be bunnies and sit on your keisters and hold your yaps. One crack out of any of you and I'll pat you with a spade." Yeah, of course I knew she was there. Do you think I'm a coward?

I sat up. "What the lady's basically saying guys is 'put your hands in the air or she'll shoot lots of holes into you. She's quick on the draw so don't be . . .' what was that one, Fifi?"

"Bunnies," said the black-clad figure with the weird eyebrows and the gun.

"Stupid?" She nodded. "So don't be stupid, and sit down and shut up or you're likely to be killed." Fifi smiled at me, like a teacher with her favourite pupil. I walked over to Stubezzi and relieved him of his dinky little gun.

"Who the hell is this?" said Aurora, "And why does she look like Joan Crawford on acid?"

I was about to answer but Fifi beat me to it. "Calm it, sister. You'd better get your flaps down or you'll take off. We could bump gums all day, chippy. I'm the triggerman so close your head, ya big palooka, and grab air unless you want to say hello to the Undertaker's Friend here." She gestured with her head at the gun in her hand.

Aurora looked at me. I shrugged. "You're on your own with that one. I don't have a clue. But I don't think it was very complimentary."

"Drop a dime to the flatfoots, Helena, so they can give 'em the third in stir."

"Ummmmmmmmmm, nope, sorry Fifi, run that one by me again?"

She nodded in the direction of the telephone. "The cops."

"Oh, right." I walked over to the desk, laid the gun down and picked up the phone but as I turned my back Evan Stubezzi launched himself at Fifi, knocking the gun out of her hand. As they both dived for it, Aurora grabbed at the gun I'd put on the desk. Fifi managed to keep hold of her weapon but Stubezzi spotted the big black gun which Smilla had relinquished earlier. Within seconds, Fifi had a gun which she was pointing at Stubezzi, Stubezzi had a gun which he was pointing at Aurora, and Aurora had a gun which she was pointing at Fifi. I think this was what was known as a Mexican standoff. I would have felt more comfortable if I had been holding something a tad more dangerous than a telephone receiver. Smilla was standing white-faced, clutching her bleeding arm.

They all stood there, pointing stuff at each other. Evan Stubezzi was sweating, and with the hand that wasn't holding the gun he lowered the zip of his Armani jacket. Since when did Armani suit jackets have zips? Of course, Evan Stubezzi and his pathological fear of buttons. Damn, if I'd noticed the zip a few hours earlier, we wouldn't be in this mess now.

"Anybody mind if I get myself a drink?" My left hand went towards the drawer. Fifi nodded almost imperceptibly. She knew what I was going to do. I slowly reached my hand in, pulled out a bottle of tequila and a couple of glasses. "Anyone want some?" I held up the bottle and clinked the glasses together. The sound made them all look at me. "No? Sure?"

Quickly, I flung the bottle towards Stubezzi who turned his gun in the direction of the flying bottle and fired. The bullet went wide and clanged into the filing cabinet about 6 feet away from me. I knew then that I'd made a mistake. He couldn't shoot for toffee. I should have aimed at Aurora who had the fastest reactions. She stood there, legs spread, gun in hand, calm as a cucumber that's never been in a small private investigator's office full of people shooting. That's a small office, not a small private investigator, by the way. She was aiming straight at me and I dived out of the way just in time. A bullet smacked into the wall right behind where I had been standing. If I'd been a couple of seconds slower, my brains would have decorated the wall like a bad Jackson Pollock. Or even a good Jackson Pollock.

Within seconds the air was full of the smell of . . . that stuff inside bullets. The noise was deafening and the bullets were flying around like . . . well . . . like bullets. I'm sorry, but the moment was just too tense for me to think of any good similes. I was too busy trying to stay alive. And, to add insult to injury, all my lovely shiny new electronic equipment was exploding around my ears. The only piece of kit that would have been of use—the flashlight stun gun—was in pieces on the floor. The infrared thermometer and the hot dog grill and bun warmer were the only things still in one piece on the shelves. Even if I could have reached them I would only have been able to take Aurora's temperature and warm Stubezzi's buns. What the hell use was that at a time like this? I couldn't even video the whole thing and send it off to 'You've Been Framed'. The camcorder was crushed under Smilla's feet as she stumbled around like a bull in a bullet-ridden china shop, trying to get out of the way.

My already small office felt smaller than a toilet cubicle. I didn't like being at a disadvantage but, without a gun, that's exactly what I was at. No gun, just bottles of booze in a drawer I couldn't reach. Plus, one of my sore legs was playing up. I needed another painkiller, and they were in the same drawer as the booze. Through the smoke and haze that lay over the room like a tramp's blanket (see what I can do when there's a momentary lull?), I saw Stubezzi's legs and decided to go for them to see if I could topple him. I crouched and launched myself at his legs, shouting, "Evan! Look out for the shiny buttons!" Unfortunately, it didn't have the desired effect. Instead of freezing and looking around for the buttons, he screamed and discharged a hail of bullets. I ducked, shouts and bangs and bullets whizzing past me in all directions.

I heard the warning from Fifi, but reacted too slowly. When she said, "Dive," I thought she was talking about the state of the place. I didn't realise she was actually telling me to dive. It seemed too straightforward for Fifi. As a result, I caught a bullet in the arm. It slammed me back against the desk and the impact took my breath away, leaving me a sitting duck while I tried to forget the pain and pull myself together. As Aurora took aim again, I rolled away and felt a second bullet plough into the soft, fleshy part of my upper leg. OK, it was my buttock. And it stung like hell.

I staggered to my feet, another bullet catching me in the shoulder. I collapsed to the floor. I could feel the blood pumping from my wounds. The noises in the room started to sound as though they were being strained through an earful of treacle, and I was feeling light-headed.

The last thing I heard before I blacked out was Fifi shrieking, "You fucking screwy twist, you've sent my dollface for the Big Sleep." She sounded distraught. Her face appeared above me. Darkness was starting to close in but I knew it was Fifi. A false eyelash lay on her cheek like a depressed spider, the bee stung scarlet lips were quivering, and the Joan Crawford eyebrows were locked in a tortured embrace as she frowned. I wanted to tell her not to worry, that I wasn't going for the Big Sleep, I just wanted a little nap. But I was too tired.

CHAPTER SIXTEEN

(It's Just A Scratch)

I was dreaming. A pair of severed hands clad in white gloves was using my skull as a drum kit. Banging away at The Ramones' 'Sheena Is a Punk Rocker' over and over again. The drum kit had a name painted on the side—The Serial Killers—with a picture of a red fish. We were on *Top Of The Pops* and hundreds of screaming teenagers were dressed as Pekinese dogs with red and green bows in their topknots. Along the side of the stage perched the three wise monkeys: See No Evil, Hear No Evil and Speak No Evil. I didn't know where I was. Why did *Top Of The Pops* feel just like being buried in a big, warm cushiony marshmallow? I took a big bite out of the marshmallow and coughed. One of the three wise monkeys loomed over me from a great . . . no, from a height, and said, "She's coming round." Somewhere from the depths of my subconscious something was nagging at me. I was chasing an enormous red balloon which had 'clue' written on it in big letters, but it was just out of reach. I needed to tell one of the three wise monkeys something important, but I didn't know what it was. The balloon faded into the distance and then popped, soundlessly; the three wise monkeys disappeared and the marshmallow enfolded me again in its sweet-smelling, sugary depths.

When I woke up again, it appeared that a whole family of cats had used my mouth as a litter tray while I'd slept. My head felt as though somebody was stomping on it with hobnail boots, my shoulder was throbbing and someone seemed to be giving my left bum cheek a rather nasty going over with a hot poker. The marshmallow had turned into a hospital bed in which I seemed to be strapped down, and the three wise monkeys were still sitting beside me.

I tried to open my eyes, but someone had glued my eyelids in place—presumably the same person who had let loose a hive of angry bees inside my skull. I wanted to get hold of that person and make them pay. I didn't feel well, and someone was going to suffer for it later. I was hoping it wasn't going to be me.

I lay there in the marshmallow depths, strong lights beating into my closed eyelids and making me determined to keep them closed a while longer. The room was warm and stuffy. After a while the buzzing in my head gradually sorted itself out into something I could make sense of. The three wise monkeys were talking.

"God, what if she never comes out of it? It's all my fault. I should never have asked her to take the case. If only I hadn't gone round there waving my brother's hands."

"It's no good blaming yourself. She's a grown woman and a damn stubborn one at that. I told her I don't know how many times to keep her goddam nose out of police business, but did she listen? Hell, no. And now I've got the guv'nor on my ass for involving a civilian in a police investigation. Shit, no wonder I've got ulcers and four ex-wives and a grumpy demeanour."

"By heck, she's a fine looking lass and no mistake. Even wi' that pale face and all those bandages, and the fartin' and snorin'. Do you think I should give her a bed bath? Save the nurses the bother, an' all that?"

Now would be as good a time as any to open my eyes. I wanted to say something profound, something that would make them all burst into tears and marvel at my bravery. I said, "I'm going to throw up."

Frank Lee barrelled out of the room bellowing, "Nurse!" Owen Banks fetched me one of those little cardboard hats they give you in hospital to be sick into, and Hal Litosis sucked his false teeth in and out a few times.

Frank came running back in, followed by the white-coated doctor I had seen on my first visit to Casualty—could it be only a couple of days before? He stuck a thermometer in my mouth and took hold of my wrist.

"How long have I been here?"

"Six days." He checked the drip going into my left hand.

"Oh gny Ga. I neeg oo et uk. Nere's Hihi?" I took the thermometer out of my mouth and tried again. "Oh my God. I need to get up. Where's Fifi? Is she alive? What about Virgil? Has anyone been feeding him?"

"The Roman poet?" The doctor pushed me gently back down on the bed. "He's been dead for just over two thousand years. It's just the concussion talking. Let's see your temperature." He took the thermometer from my hand and put it back in my mouth."

"She means her cat," said Frank Lee. "Don't worry, Helena. Fifi's been feeding him and cleaning his box. And she's fine, by the way. The hero of the hour, in fact. After you got shot she turned into something out of Revenge Of The Mutant Joan Crawford Ninja Turtles. If I've translated correctly, she spun on one leg and kicked Stubezzi in the chin, winged Aurora with a well-placed bullet, and punched Smilla in the nose. By the time the police and ambulance arrived, she had all three of them trussed up like oven-ready chickens and was cradling you in her arms, having sucked out one of the bullets, and was staunching the bloodflow from your wounds. She saved your life."

I made a mental note to give her a pay rise. As well as a big hug. She was definitely the best psycho sidekick a private eye ever had. A thought struck me. I removed the thermometer from my mouth again and handed it to the doctor. "Which bullet did she suck out, doc?"

"The one in your arm," the doctor said, frowning as he read my temperature. "The one in your shoulder went straight through. We just plugged up the hole."

"And what about the one in my . . . errrr . . . upper thigh?" I gave Hal Litosis a glare as he sniggered.

The doctor shrugged. "We poked about a bit in there but couldn't find it. Buried too deep, I guess."

Great, not only did I have a complex about the size of my nose, but my arse had taken on such enormous proportions that it could not only stop a speeding bullet but swallow it up in some sort of cellulite black hole.

"It's a nice clean wound though, lass."

I glared at Hal. Again. "And you would know this how, exactly?"

He had the grace to look embarrassed. "Aye, well, so the doctor says, like."

"When can I get out of here? I need to get back to work. I have a serial killer and thirty million in stolen diamonds to find." I struggled to sit up. Frank's eyebrows drew together like two horny caterpillars. "For the police," I added hurriedly. "I need to help the police find the serial killer and the diamonds."

The doctor checked his chart. "I'm sorry, but I can't let you out for at least three weeks. You've lost seven pints of blood, have multiple gunshot wounds and re-fractured both your arms. You've broken all the ribs that weren't broken before, we've replaced your left hip joint and your collarbone is crushed. And we had to re-set your nose. You should give up boxing by the way. Oh, and your liver's not in the best of shape, and your cholesterol is way too high."

I looked at Owen. "Fetch my clothes."

"Really, you must stay here, Miss Handbasket. You're not strong enough." I was beginning to dislike this doctor.

"Just give me one of those release forms and I'll sign it and be on my way. If you could see your way clear to giving me a prescription for some mild painkillers that would be good too. And a couple of Band-Aids."

"Oh well, if you insist."

The doctor went off to get the form and I asked Frank Lee for an update on the case. While I'd been tucked up in my hospital bed, Stubezzi, DeGreasepaint and DaCrowde had all been arrested and essentially admitted to everything they'd said in my office. The two women had been charged with assault, attempted murder, threatening behaviour, various firearms offences and breach of the peace; Evan Stubezzi had been charged with corporate fraud, assault, attempted murder, perverting the course of justice, impersonating an FBI agent and speaking in a really bad American accent. So far, none of them had owned up to the serial killings. Frank Lee was convinced that one or all of them had been the serial killer, although he was basing his assumption on the somewhat flimsy fact that there hadn't been another killing since they'd been arrested six days ago. I wasn't convinced.

Before I could argue, however, a new arrival burst into the hospital room. "Dollface! Man, we were in a jam and you took the Broderick. I thought you was zotzed, but you look hotcha, as though you're hitting on all eight and that's flat."

I wasn't quite up to Fifi-speak, but luckily there was help from a surprising source. Hal stepped up and put his arm around Fifi. "She says you were all in big trouble and you took a hell of a beating. She thought you were dead, but you look great and as though you're in good shape and that's for sure."

I glanced from one to the other and Hal added, "We've been pitching woo and I'm dizzy with the dame."

Oh my God, now there was another of them. Fifi blushed. "He says we've been seeing each other and he's madly in love with me." I stared at her for a long moment, trying not to imagine her in Hal's office, pitching some woo over his desk as he warbled a medley of James Brown numbers in her shell-like, his teeth clicking romantically. Too late, I'd already imagined it, and it was going to take a long time to recover from the trauma.

The doctor returned and I signed the forms and hopped out of bed.

I had a few aches and pains but nothing that a good sleep, a hot shower, and a couple of Stingers (three ounces of brandy, one and a half ounces of white crème de menthe, poured over ice) wouldn't cure. The doctor handed me a bottle of painkillers, some Band-Aids and a yellow and pink spotted rubber ring. "Here, you might need this. For the . . . errr . . . upper thigh wound."

"Cheers, doc. See you soon."

"I do hope not." He strode off, his white coat flapping.

"Oh, doc." He turned to face me. "What does your wife think about you extracting bullets from the upper thighs of strange women?"

"She doesn't mind. She's a nurse."

Damn.

Frank Lee dropped me off at home, having lectured me all the way. According to him, the serial killer, or killers, had been caught, and I should forget about the whole thing now, and get a proper career. Yeah, right. Who sacked my mother and gave the job to Frank?

"Sorry, Frank, but after I get something to eat, and have a quick nap, I'm getting straight back to work. There's a little voice nagging at me, telling me I need to go and see Charity Case and Emma Roids again. One of them knows something, I'm sure of it." I just hoped that I wouldn't be too late.

Lee growled at me. "Look, Helena, just leave it alone, will you? We've questioned Charity Case over and over and we're still getting nothing. Lou Gubrious is heading round to question Emma Roids again, but the chances are he'll learn nothing new. Face it, the case is solved and either one of the sisters or Evan Stubezzi is the serial killer. We may never know the full truth."

I shrugged and limped into the house. Virgil was lying on the sofa, cleaning his face. He paused in mid-wash, looked at me as though to say, "Oh, it's you," jumped off the sofa, and stalked into the kitchen.

I followed him in and opened the fridge. I was sure that there wouldn't be anything in there, and even if there was, it would be inedible by now, but I had a quick look anyway. I dredged up a few bits and pieces. I could maybe fling together a fricassee of scallops and tiger prawns with Pernod and crème fraiche sauce, served with lemon grass, baby corncobs and julienne of carrots and green beans. I slung everything into a pan and turned the cooker on. Virgil had been messing in his litter tray and had kicked cat litter all over the floor.

He was sitting looking at the jumbled pile of litter expectantly and meowing.

I must still have been woozy from all the bullets and the drugs because it looked as though the spilled litter had formed letters which had bizarrely joined together to spell out:

THIS SERIAL KILLER STUFF ISN'T OVER UNTIL THE FAT LADY SINGS, YOU KNOW. BE CAREFUL—DON'T GO DOWN ANY DARK ALLEYS WITHOUT A GUN AND A TORCH. OH, AND BY THE WAY, CAN YOU GET FIFI TO DO SOMETHING ABOUT THOSE EYEBROWS?

I must be hallucinating. I shook my head to clear it.

"Virgil, old son, it is, quite literally, a pain in the arse for me to bend down, so please try and be a little neater, would you?" I swept up the cat litter and dished up my scallops and prawns, serving it with a Sidecar (an ounce of brandy, two thirds of an ounce of cointreau, two thirds of an ounce of fresh lemon juice, shaken, not stirred.)

After a quick shower, I changed into camouflage trousers, khaki t-shirt and a pair of Docs. Today I meant business. Besides, the camos were easy on the rear and I could pad them out with some nice soft bandages without it looking like I had a fat arse.

I drove to the office. Fifi, bless her, had had the glass in the door fixed again, and the sign was freshly painted: 'Handbasket and Fofum—Partners In Crime—No Case Solved'. No Case Solved? What was that—truth in advertising or something?

I opened the door. Fifi had been busy in the last few days. The mismatched chairs and battered desk had been replaced by two (yes, two) smaller, smarter desks—one in each corner, flanking the door that led to the tiny room where Fifi used to sit when she was my secretarial support. Each of the desks had a brass nameplate: 'Helena Handbasket—PI' and 'Fifi Fofum—Psycho Sidekick'. At each desk was one of those whirly chairs that I'd coveted for a long while. There were two other chairs, smaller, and non-whirly—for clients, I presumed—and a small sofa along one wall. All the seats were upholstered in a matching print fabric that, from where I was standing, looked like little tiny smoking guns on a pale blue background. I moved closer to inspect one of the chairs. Yes, that's exactly what it was. Curtains in the same fabric hung at the now sparkling window, from which the broken blind had been removed. Where was my battered and traditional PI office? Where were my dust motes floating lazily in the sun that sneaked in through the slatted Venetian blinds? Where was my sodding secretary?

"Dollface!" Fifi appeared from the room at the back of the office. Her eyebrows were on fine form, but I hardly noticed them for the suit. She was wearing one of her black '40's suits with the pencil skirt and enormous shoulder pads—she had to turn sideways to get through the door to come and hug me—but the lapels and cuff trims, and the buttons, were covered in the smoking gun fabric. She mistook my look of horror for one of awe and gave me a twirl.

Hal Litosis appeared behind her, red lipstick covering his face. "Eh up, lass. What do ya think?" he waved an expansive hand. "Me and Fifi did it up as a surprise. Fifi sewed all the stuff herself, while she were sitting in the hospital waiting for you to come round. Like it?"

"It's . . . gorgeous." I was touched. "But what's that sign on the door all about? 'No Case Solved?'"

"Aye, sorry about that, lass. I'd been at the hooch in your drawer, and got it a bit wrong. I were just about to paint the missing 'Un' in."

"Well, thanks for clearing up and doing all this." I sighed. "I see none of my lovely new equipment survived the carnage."

"Aye, it did." Hal held the door to the back room open a little wider. There, next to the coffee pot, stood the hot dog grill and bun warmer.

"Oh well," I said, "at least I still have the Global Positioning System."

I called Emma Roids constantly over the next quarter of an hour but her number was engaged. I needed to see her. I decided just to go round to her house and see if I could get to the bottom of what was bothering me. After saying goodbye to Fifi and Hal, I ran out to my car. I stopped dead at the kerb. Some bastard had smashed the window and nicked my GPS.

XXXXX

Emma's wrought iron gates were open so I drove in and parked in between her Porsche and a police car. Lou Gubrious must be here questioning her, as Frank had mentioned. I knocked on the door, but there was no response. Both Emma's cars were in the driveway, and I could hear the dogs yapping inside. Since she never went anywhere without them, I knew she was home. I knocked harder, and called through the letterbox but there was no response, other than the frenzied barking of the dogs.

I went round the back of the house. The pool was empty as was the sun lounger, but a half full glass (or half empty, depending on your outlook) sat next to it. The patio doors were open and I went inside, calling Emma's name.

Ruby and Emerald ran up to me, wagging their tails and yipping and then backing away. I followed them into the lounge. Emma's body lay on the Persian carpet, the handset of the phone lying next to her, beeping frantically. Her hands were still attached, and there was no small scarlet fish or biblical note, so I didn't think she was a victim of the serial killer. I felt her neck, but I already knew from the staring eyes and protruding tongue that she was dead. It looked as though she had been strangled.

I poked about a bit for clues. I couldn't find any, but I did find the body of Lou Gubrious on the kitchen floor, shot with what looked like his own gun. It lay by his body and I wondered if the poor guy had committed suicide. Maybe he couldn't face the thought of retiring in a couple of weeks. I picked up the gun and then hurriedly replaced it when I remembered that I should really leave it for the lab boys. Otherwise I'd have to explain how my fingerprints got on everything, including the murder weapon. I was a fast learner.

I picked up the phone and called Frank.

He swore and said he'd be right over. "You go home. I'll come and see you shortly. Don't touch anything and try not to stumble over any more bodies, would you?"

Well, there's gratitude for you.

I went out the same way I had come, scooping up Ruby and Emerald along the way. I couldn't leave them here.

Back home, I took the yapping dogs into the house. Virgil went into a frenzy, standing on his back legs and swiping at the dogs' noses while yowling what sounded very much like a Bee Gees song. I placed Ruby and Emerald on the sofa where they looked over the arm in horror. Virgil, now in a complete huff, was scratching at the newspaper which had been delivered that morning. He was shredding it into little pieces, scattering it everywhere. I got a dustpan and brush. The torn-up words and letters were spread out over the floor:

rats get of rid those stolen know i jewels where the are

"Virgil, they're just here for a couple of days. Be nice."

An uneasy peace descended and I waited for Frank to come round and tell me what he'd found out about Emma's murder. I heard his car drawing up about an hour later and went to let him in. Ruby and Emerald ran up to the door, growling and baring their teeth.

"What are the dogs doing here?" he said. "I wondered where they were."

"I couldn't leave them there with the d-e-a-d b-o-d-i-e-s. Come in."

"Actually, I won't, if you don't mind. I don't like dogs and they don't like me. I much prefer cats." Virgil sprinted over and started twining himself round Frank's legs, purring. "Anyway, it looks as though Emma Roids' murder is something to do with the fact that she was blackmailing several of her co-workers and acquaintances. At least, we found evidence to that effect in her house. It looks as though someone got fed up with paying out to her. Either that or Charity Case was taking revenge for her husband's affair with Emma. Lou Gubrious was probably just in the wrong place at the wrong time. Poor guy. Two weeks off collecting his pension and he walks in on a blackmail scene." Lee shook his head.

"So you're sure it's nothing to do with these missing jewels?"

"What is it with you and these jewels, Helena? According to you, every damn crime in this town has something to do with the jewel heist. Everything from serial killing to joyriding."

"And why are you so sure it doesn't?"

"Look, just butt out. This is a straightforward case of murder and blackmail, with possibly a bit of sex thrown in. Leave this one to the police, would you? It looks as though we're going to be able to clear up the serial killings and a completely unrelated murder this week. The guv'nor will be pleased. It'll really boost the crime figures."

"Well, I'm not so sure. Besides, I told you, I think I may know where the jewels are."

Frank was interested at last. "Oh yes, you *did* say something about that. I forgot. Where are they? It would be nice to wrap that one up too. The investigation has been dragging on for five years, and we're no closer to solving it, although it looks as though our serial killer offed one of the perps when he killed Robin Banks. Pure coincidence, of course."

"Oh, I think I'll keep that information to myself for a little longer, Frank."

He shrugged. "Please your bloody self then." He stomped off to the car.

The phone rang. It was Owen Banks. I could hear Tammy Wynette in the background.

"Owen? What are you doing with Tammy Wynette?"

"What? Oh, I'm in the Royal Flush. Come down, I want to show you something. I'll be in the car park."

"I'll be right there." My heart was beating. Was this a date? Was he finally going to propose? Would I be able to have sex with a bullet in my arse? I ran upstairs and dressed carefully. Bugger the pain, an occasion such as this called for full-on sex appeal. I pulled on my silver halter necked mini-dress. I hadn't worn it since some joker in a club asked me if I'd thought it was fancy dress and come as oven-ready turkey. I added a pair of strappy Jimmy Choos with heels that were so high they made my calves look like an athlete's. OK, a shot-putter's, but still. My big white-beaded handbag would go nicely with the dress, and there was even room inside for a couple of guns and my pepper spray. Excellent.

I drove down to the Royal Flush and parked next to a new BMW.

"Hi, Helena." Owen Banks was leaning on the bonnet of the aubergine-coloured Beamer.

"Is this what you wanted to show me, Owen?"

"Yep." He ran his hand proudly over the shiny paint. "It was delivered three hours ago and I brought it straight down here to celebrate. We just came out to check on it."

"We?"

"Yeah. I also want you to meet my new girlfriend, Ginger." Then I noticed the strumpet standing behind him. "Ginger Vitis, meet my private eye, Helena Handbasket."

Ginger was a waif-like brunette with huge eyes and short spiky hair. She wore no make-up and looked stunning in a leather catsuit. I hated the bitch. We nodded coolly at each other.

"Ginger, I just need to go back inside and speak to Helena about the case. Do you want to wait for me in the car?"

"Ooooh, can I drive it round the car park, Owenie?"

"Sure, babe." He tossed her the keys. "Just don't scratch it or I'll spank you."

"Mmmm, promises, promises, big boy."

I pulled his arm. "Let's get inside, *Owenie.* I need a drink before I vomit."

He gave Ginger a long lingering kiss as she opened the driver's door and I stalked off to the pub. He caught up with me at the door. "So, how are you?"

I was just about to answer when Owen's new car and girlfriend exploded. I'm not going to describe it. You've heard it before. Ho hum.

Owen shook his head. "Why does this sort of thing keep happening to me?" He held the door open and we went in.

As Owen went up to the bar I said, "Get me a beer would you, I'm just going to powder my nose." I headed towards the ladies room. As I perched over the toilet my phone rang. A muffled, rasping voice said, "Helena Handbasket?" Obviously, people around here hadn't been taking their Vitamin C. I answered in the affirmative.

"Lady, do what I say and don't say a word. Leave your Uzi and pepper spray in the toilets and come to the darkest dark alley you can find. Don't tell anyone where you're going. Be there in five minutes or Owen Banks is toast. OK? . . . OK? . . . Hey, lady, are you there?"

"Oh, I'm sorry. You said don't say a word. Righty-ho. I'll be there in five."

The voice had reminded me of someone but I couldn't quite put my finger on who. Oh well, it would come back to me at some point. As instructed I put my Uzi and my pepper spray behind the tank. He hadn't said anything about the .38, but it would make sense that if he didn't want me to take the Uzi and the pepper spray then he wouldn't want me to bring the .38, right? So I took that out of my bag too. I left the toilet, crossed to where Owen was sitting and picked up my coat. "I'm just nipping out for a few minutes. I can't tell you where I'm going or who I'm going to meet, so don't ask me."

"OK. See ya."

I left the bar and splashed across the rutted car park. These shoes were going to be absolutely ruined.

I headed along Sleazy Street until I came across the darkest alley I could find. I could barely make out the dumpsters and the rats were just scurrying blobs. Maybe this wasn't such a good idea after all. And just maybe I should have left the .38 in the handbag. I pulled my phone out of my bag to call Owen, a call that might just save my life. I switched it on and put it to my ear. Damn. It had just died. I knew I should have recharged it sometime within the last couple of months. It wasn't as though these things lasted indefinitely, right? Oh, well. Too late to worry about it now. I continued to the end of the alleyway, which was around the corner and out of sight of any casual passers-by.

A dark shadow appeared at the entrance of the alley and a figure loomed towards me. I squeaked in fear.

"Not so brave now, are you, missy?"

Of course. I knew that voice now. It was Detective Lee. I should have known from the moment I laid eyes on him that he was a crooked cop. He was carrying a gun. I wasn't sure what brand, but it was large and menacing, just like Lee himself. He gestured for me to put my hands behind my head and spread 'em. A very precise piece of gesturing. I would have liked him on my team during Charades.

"Are you going to kill me?" I asked him. "I thought we were getting along really well. I had you down as husband material. Just shows you how wrong a girl can be."

"I don't have much time, and I want to reveal to you all the details of my evil plan. Before I kill you."

He laid it out for me. How he'd been in Stubezzi's pocket from the start, like a tame but grumpy hamster. I asked him how he hadn't recognised Evan Stubezzi when he was disguised as Agent Art Ifarti, but he said he was thrown by the sunglasses and the fake American accent. After the jewellery heist Frank had been chasing Robin Banks—ostensibly on behalf of Stubezzi, but with the intention of double-crossing him. Frank had found Robin first, holed up in a motel in Milton Keynes. He had tortured him and forced him to write the note to Owen, thinking that Owen was in on the heist (right) and that he knew where the jewels were (wrong). Before Robin could tell Lee where the jewels were, he'd died from Lee's over-enthusiastic torturing. The story took longer to tell when Lee was narrating it but I've shortened it and fixed the grammar. He was a really bad storyteller.

Lee had concocted the serial killer cover to throw both the cops and Stubezzi off the scent. "I figured that if they thought they were looking for a serial killer, then they wouldn't think this had anything to do with the jewels. I don't know much about the Bible, but I know the Ten Commandments, so I wrote 'Thou Shalt Not Steal' on a piece of paper and stuffed it in his mouth. I cut off Robin's hands because I know that serial killers usually take a trophy from their victims, but in the end, I couldn't bring himself to pick up the hands, so I left them there." He paused. "I was really surprised when the body didn't turn up, and even more surprised when Owen ended up with the hands."

"What about the others?" I was trying to buy myself time while I came up with a brilliant escape plan. At the moment, I couldn't really give a toss about the others.

"From what Robin had said I knew Luke Warmwater was involved. I thought he might know where the jewels were. He didn't, but pointed me to Justin Case, mistakenly thinking it was Justin who was blackmailing him, rather than Justin's mistress, because Emma had written to him using Justin's headed notepaper. Of course, that led *me* to believe it was Justin, too, rather than Emma. So I killed them both. I had to continue with the serial killer, hand-chopping, biblical thing. It was easy to come up with a Commandment to fit Justin, but the Luke Warmwater one was a bit of a stretch."

I remembered the posters of David Beckham at Luke Warmwater's flat and the Commandment about Gods and idols. "And what about my poor, barking neighbour?"

"Well, I started tailing you once you became involved and realised that your neighbour was completely bonkers and a religious maniac, so I thought I could throw suspicion on him. Unfortunately, the plan backfired, and he had to go. By that time, I couldn't be arsed with the Commandments stuff, so I made one up."

So I was right. 'Thou Shalt Not Keep Body Parts in A Fridge In The Basement' definitely wasn't one of the Ten Commandments.

"And as for Emma Roids, well, she had been snooping around Stubezzi's office the day Aurora deGreasepaint and Smilla daCrowde had paid him a visit to tell him about the jewel heist and that they knew where Robin Banks was. After they'd gone, he rang me, and told me he was going to the motel to get the jewels from Banks. As you know, I got there before Stubezzi. Only, I found out later, not before Emma Roids. She had listened in to my phone conversation with Stubezzi at his office and gone to see Robin. She told him we were after him and persuaded him he'd be safer giving up the jewels to her, and that she would get him another safe house. I found that all out from her, but she made me so mad that I strangled her before she could tell me where the jewels were. The thing is, I would never have known about her, because Robin didn't say anything. But after two of her blackmail victims were murdered, she was casting her net wider for more. She knew I was crooked, so she contacted me. I went round there and she tried to blackmail me. Poor old Lou just happened to walk in on us as I was strangling her. I'd forgotten he was going round to question her some more. Oh well, at least we didn't have to buy him a retirement present."

I remembered the note I had found in Emma's office, with the list of potential new victims. I had thought that the notation 'Police?' had meant she was worried about them finding out, when in fact she had been planning to blackmail one of them.

He cocked the gun. "So, that's basically it. I feel better for telling someone. And now I have you. And you're going to tell me where the jewels are."

"One last question. What about the scarlet fish in the chest cavity? What was the significance of that?"

"No significance, just one of those unexplained red herrings. Now, tell me where the jewels are."

I had by now formulated my brilliant escape plan. "Of course I'll tell you. Come closer though, I need to whisper it to you." As Lee stepped towards me I spun and kicked out at him with one of my pointy-shoed feet. I caught him between the legs and he fell to the floor like a big fat crooked policeman who's been kicked in the nuts. As he fell he dropped his gun and I picked it up and clubbed him with the butt. He was out cold. I took his handcuffs and cuffed him to the railing at the end of the alleyway. Well, *that* was easy.

I ran back to the bar and found Owen. "Quick, we need to find an honest cop. I'm not sure how easy that's going to be. Come on, we'll have to go in my car since yours is burnt to a crisp."

At the police station we set out the whole story for a disbelieving and shaken Chief Inspector Angus Beef. I explained the whole thing to him and told him where he could pick up his murderous subordinate.

Owen was silent as I drove him home. "So what about the jewels?" he said as we pulled up outside his house.

"I'll explain it all to you tomorrow after I've had a good night's sleep."

XₒXₒXₒXₒXₒ

The next day, I turned up at Owen's house with a yapping Ruby and Emerald, none the worse for having spent the night with Virgil. Virgil, on the other hand, had disappeared.

Owen looked shocked to see the dogs. "Why have you brought *them?*"

I smiled smugly. "Because the dogs are called Ruby and Emerald." He looked at me blankly. "Emma Roids, blackmailer extraordinaire, knew too much for her own good. She got hold of the jewels, and gave them to her pampered pooches for safekeeping. Look at their collars." As I held the dogs up, the gems on their collars twinkled in the sunlight. Not diamante after all, but the real thing.

A car drew up outside. There was a knock at the door. Owen went outside for a few minutes and when he returned he was brandishing a set of keys. "My new BMW. Fancy giving it a test drive while I divest Ruby and Emerald of their precious cargos?"

"I'd love to," I said as I grabbed the key from him. He gave me a firm kiss on the lips and I went out to the car.

As I turned the key in the ignition, it struck me that there was still one loose, unexplained thread. We never had discovered who had been planting explosives in Owen Banks' cars. No matter, at some point it would come to me in a flash.

Printed in the United States
52860LVS00002B/31-39